Executioner

S L Davies

Published by S L Davies, 2022.

EXECUTIONER

First edition. December 4, 2022.

Copyright © 2022 S L Davies.

ISBN: 979-8215445044

Written by S L Davies.

Chapter One

"That's right baby, right down your throat," Maverick or better known as X, which stood for Executioner, groaned.

He looked down at the cute brunette with her big brown eyes that was currently sucking his cock down her throat, gagging as it hit the back of her tonsils. His balls were tightening with every thrust into her mouth. X roared out as he filled her mouth with hot spurts of cum, the girl's eyes watered as he held her head tight to his pelvis, forcing her to drink every last drop. Once his cock stopped twitching, X released the back of the girl's head and leaned against the wall. The girl wiped her bottom lip and looked up at him with hope in her eyes.

The girls always looked at him with that same look, a look that pleaded for X to make them his. However, it was the same story for every one of them. They were no more than a hot pussy or mouth, occasionally he found one who would be willing to give up her ass, but at the end of the day, it was about his pleasure. They could go and find one of the other guys in the club if they wanted cuddles and romance. That wasn't X.

There was a reason he was the executioner. The sergeant at arms of his MC, The Kingsmen. He didn't give a fuck about anything. His life was lived hard and fast. He was quick to pull the trigger of his sawn-off shotgun, he fucked hard and his brothers were the only ones that got his heart and trust. There had been many men and a few women who had seen the barrel end of his shotgun, there were none that lived to tell about it.

"X? Will you make me cum?" the brunette on her knees asked with a nasally whine while looking up at him with her big begging eyes.

X smirked and chuckled, "go find one of the prospects, I'm betting they will be wanting to give you all you need."

The girl's eyes widened, he kept calling her the girl in his head, because the truth was when she told him her name, he hadn't bothered listening, it didn't matter to him. He preferred his women to not talk. He looked down at her with a raised eyebrow as he tucked his now flaccid cock back in his jeans. She frowned and growled as she stood up from her knees, as she spun on her heel, she flicked him in the chest with her hair.

X reached out and snagged her hair in his hand, spinning her back to face him with a squeal. Her eyes watered from the hold he had on her. "Lose the fucking attitude," he growled, before releasing her.

The girl gave a quick nod, before she turned, this time without attitude and headed over to their latest prospect, Hale. The kid was green, X had been against him prospecting for the club, but it had been ultimately the President, Blaine's decision and what he said, was law. So, Hale became a prospect. He was more tolerable than when he first joined them. Hale needed experience. He was a street kid that had run away from junkie parents and found himself outside the club house. Angel, Blaine's old lady took pity on him and brought Hale to Blaine. There was only one person that could get Blaine to lose his hardened exterior and that was his old lady. So, when Angel asked Blaine to bring the kid in, Hale was brought in. He was a pain in the ass and X was ready to kill the shit, but once he got his end wet between the thighs of Hadley, one of the club girls, he calmed down, all the extra testosterone that he was throwing down, left him out the eye of his cock. Hale was better off for it, Hadley now made sure to keep him well supplied by the club whores, who regularly serviced the guys.

Hadley was a red head who had been with them what seemed like forever. She looked like she could be in her fifties, but the truth was X had no idea how old she was. She trained the girls, cooked for the guys and was generally the mama bear of the club. She normally didn't fuck the guys of the club and the guys respected her decision, but she had a soft spot for Hale, she wanted to man him up. There was no room for weakness in a club like theirs. So, she had taken him back to her room and fucked him every which way to Sunday. The boy came out red faced and wearing a grin the size of Texas. The club cheered and patted him on the back as he came to the bar, where their bartender, Johnny poured him a shot of whiskey and told him it would put hair on the kid's chest. Hale sucked it down in one gulp, before his whole body was taken over by hacking coughs. Hale patted his chest and looked around the room, his eyes watering as he gasped for air. The guys at the bar laughed like a pack of hyenas. Truth was, they all did that the first time Johnny poured them a shot of whiskey, it was as strong as fucking rocket fuel.

Johnny distilled his own whiskey, one of their side businesses was moonshine and whiskey, that Johnny made. He'd been making it for years; his daddy and his granddaddy had made it before him and passed down the recipe. From what X knew his granddaddy had been the bartender for the club also. X grew up with Johnny and remembered hanging out with him at the club with his father. X's father was sergeant at arms of the club also, and when he was killed in action, five years prior, it became X's job to step up and take his place. For the first year and a bit, he had made it his job to seek revenge on every fucker that had been involved in the death of his father. Starting with the president of The Iron Horsemen. X tortured that piece of shit for three days straight before he gave up and died.

The Iron Horsemen had always been their enemies, they wanted the turf that The Kingsmen owned. They were always trying to shovel their low-class party drugs on their turf. And every time they were found out, The Kingsmen would take them out, usually at the hand of X. However, they never learned. The Iron Horsemen were like a multifaced snake, you lop the head off one and there is another to replace them. Most of the time, they were the sons of the previous Pres., they bred like fucking rabbits. They had club whores coming out the woodwork and usually they were kept barefoot and pregnant.

X didn't have much love for women, especially the club whores, however, even he drew the line at treating the women the way they did. It wasn't unusual to see one of their women in town with a busted lip or black eyes. The kids all had a wide-eyed stare of terror. They ran the place like a fucking cult. You had to be born into the club to join, and as far as X knew, no one ever left. The common joke was that they had to have run out of fresh blood by now, surely sisters and brothers were fucking. It sent a shudder through X at the thought of it.

Normally the cops would stop them, CPS would be called, and that shit would be shut down, but like The Kingsmen, The Iron Horsemen had the cops in their back pockets. No one else was brave enough to report them, and if CPS rocked up, who would protect them? Not the cops. So, the abuse and shit that X didn't even want to think about continued to happen. X looked over his club, Blaine had his old lady, Angel on his lap, his fingers played in her pants, their VP, Gannon, sat watching Arsen, one of the prospects and Diesel play pool. Random bikers were dotted throughout the room, club whores were on their knees or dancing for the men. Hadley was cleaning up empty cups and laughing at the guys antics. The girl that had X's cock down her throat only minutes earlier seemed to be over her upset, while Hale had her on her back and his head buried between her thighs. Her high-pitched squeals making X's back teeth ache.

Chapter Two

"Hey X, did Paige take care of you well enough?" Lolly, one of the whores that had been with the club for a few years asked.

X looked down at Lolly and raised his eyebrow, "Paige?" he asked.

Lolly rolled her eyes and chuckled, "the girl who sucked the cum from your dick, seriously X, if your cock wasn't so pretty, you wouldn't be worth the hassle."

X shrugged and chuckled, he didn't give a shit what the girls thought of him. There was no way he was going to make any of them an old lady, which was ultimately what they all wanted. He was happy dipping his cock in them and then going to bed alone. He didn't need a woman to cuddle. Fuck he lost his virginity when he was twelve to a club whore on the pool table. He had to fucking stand on a chair just to reach her pussy with his cock, she showed him how to pleasure a woman. He fucked her every day and night until he was fifteen, when she was found raped, beaten and killed, out the front of the club, dumped on the side of the road like a piece of garbage. X was devastated, he cried, when his dad saw the tears, he took his son and pulled him into his chest.

"Our first love always hurts the fucking most," his dad had said quietly, "but you're a man, you wipe off your tears, you pull your shoulders back, and you take your sorrow and turn it into the anger you are going to need to fuck a man up, you understand me?"

It was the very next day that X tortured and killed his first man. It turned out that when Bree had left the club to go home, she had been followed by one of The Iron Horsemen. He wasn't even one of the guys in the inner circle, just some outsider muscle. When she unlocked her house, he punched her in the face and dragged into her bedroom, where he raped and beat her to death, before leaving her on their doorstep.

His dad had brought him to the warehouse they use for this sort of shit, at the back of the old disused rail yard. There tied up and spread eagled in the center of the warehouse was Martino, his girl's killer. When his dad told X who the man was, X had sneered and asked his dad if he could kill him. His dad clapped him on the back and laughed.

"You hear that boys? My boy is about to become a fucking man," he roared.

Blaine's father, who was the President of the club before Blaine, smiled a toothless smile and nodded, before he pat X on the back. Timmy, Blaine's father, pointed to the bag that held X's father's gear, "alright son, as long as it's good with your old man, go for it. Let me give you a rundown of how this works. First, I will ask him a question, if I like his answer, then I won't let you hurt him, however, if I don't like his answer, then I want you to cut him deep, wherever on the body you like, just don't kill him. We need to take this slow, got it?"

X nodded his head, "yeah, got it," he said almost salivating with excitement. He could practically taste the man's blood, pumping through his veins with fear.

"Here you go son, I can't tell you how proud I am of you boy," X's father said with a grin.

X rose about another three feet with his dad's praise and smiled, nodding his head, taking the knife in his hand. A nice long bowie knife, his father held a sawn-off shotgun, the same one that became X's the day he died.

"Ya ready Mav?" Timmy called over his shoulder.

He was Maverick back then, he didn't get named Executioner until he became the sergeant at arms, it was Timmy who had bestowed him with the name. It had been X's father's name before his, so X was proud to wear it. X nodded his head and stepped up to where Timmy stood with his giant arms folded across his expansive chest. Looking at Martino, X could see that he had already had a going over, obviously at the hands of his father. Martino's eyes were almost swollen shut and some of his teeth were at his feet. His lip was busted.

"Martino, I want you to meet the Executioner's boy. The girl that you decided to take, the girl that wasn't yours to take, she was Mav here's girl. The bible says an eye for an eye, isn't that right Martino?" Timmy sneered.

Martino lifted his head and looked over to where X and Timmy stood. He pulled his head back, before spitting a globule of blood and phlegm at the feet of X. Timmy, shook his head and sighed.

"Wrong thing to do, Martino. Go ahead Mav," he said.

X stepped up to the chained man, who lifted his head and looked at X with swollen eyes. He curled his lip and sneered, "she had a nice tight pussy, until I was finished with her. By the time I was done she was so loose after she had my whole fucking fist in her."

X growled and slammed the knife into Martino's shoulder. Martino howled in pain and his head slumped forward. X slid the knife back out of his shoulder, causing Martino to scream again. X's pulse spiked with excitement, it was a euphoria that he had never experienced before, even sex, this gave him a different thrill. Not a sexual thrill, he wasn't hard, but by fuck he enjoyed himself.

They tortured Martino for four hours, before X's father put his shotgun into X's hand, "now son, the reason we use a shotgun rather than a pistol, is less ballistics. A bullet will always leave a trail, if we use the shotgun, the pellets are harder to get evidence from."

X raised the shotgun and tucked it into his shoulder. It wasn't his first time shooting a gun, he just had never shot a person before. He held the gun steady and looked down the barrel. With one eye closed he lined up the center of Martino's head, and pulled the trigger, feeling the kick against his shoulder. Martino's head snapped back as the back of his head exploded into the air and the front of his face became a mass of meat and sinew.

"Great shot son," his father crooned, before taking the gun from his hands.

X grinned like a loon at his father. In that moment he felt closer to his old man, than he ever had. Nothing like killing some fucker to bring family closer together.

Chapter Three

Lolly had given up trying to talk to X as he got lost in his head and navigated the memories that flooded his brain. When he snapped back to reality, he saw that she was bouncing on one of the guys who they called Satan, her head thrown back and her lips parted in passion. Some days X couldn't believe the debauchery that went on in the club. However, then there were days like when his dad had died or when Blaine's father passed on, that the club pulled together and debauchery was left behind, while they grieved. This family was the only family he had.

"Fuck, Blaine, Gannon, X," Arsen the prospect called from the front doors.

Their heads all snapped up to where Arsen hollered. Blaine stood, gently placing Angel on the seat he vacated, Gannon didn't give the girl he was with quite the same decency as he popped his cock out of her mouth and shoved it still hard into his jeans. They went to the door that Arsen had walked back out of. When he reappeared, he had a naked girl in his arms, she was unconscious, her head slumped back, her face unrecognizable under all the bruises. Her hair was matted with blood and she was barefoot.

"Shit, is she one of ours?" Gannon asked beside him.

X searched the girls face, he couldn't place who she was, he shook his head and sighed, reaching out and taking the girl from Arsen and leading her back towards his room. Memories flooded his mind of finding Bree in the same condition, he had to steady his breathing and allow his heart rate to reduce as he was assaulted with the awful thoughts, throwing back to fifteen.

"Doc, we are going to need you on this one," he called as he left the main bar and headed down the hallway to where the bedrooms were situated. X was the only one that currently lived at the clubhouse. Not because he couldn't get a place of his own, he just felt more comfortable there.

X laid the girl down out on his bed, she was a tiny thing, not much taller than five foot. In comparison to his large six five, she was dwarfed. She was petite and underneath the blood he could tell her hair was blonde. Her eyes were swollen, she had a hard lump on her forehead and her cheek on the left side of her face appeared to be broken. On her hairline she had a large cut, and her left eyebrow was split. Her lips were bruised, cut and swollen. Whoever had done this to her had meant to hurt her, if not kill her.

"Where was she?" he asked over his shoulder to Arsen.

"Just behind the bin, I went out for a smoke and she was lying there crumpled in a pile. At first, I thought it was a doll or just trash, until I got closer and realized it was a fucking girl," Arsen replied with a shake of his head, his voice was gravelly, and he sounded like he was struggling.

One decree the club had, is they might treat the women like shit, and not give them their hearts, they weren't soft, gentle men, however, they would never lay a violent hand to a woman. It was true that X in his time, had, had to kill a couple of women. It wasn't something he was proud of and their death always was swift. He ground his teeth, his anger and fury rising at the thought of the weak bastard that could do this to any woman.

"Get the girls in here, see if any of them recognize her? Maybe Hadley. We will need her or Angel to clean her up once Doc is done anyway," X said giving directions to the prospects.

Doc straighten her on the bed, her ribs were bruised, and she looked malnourished, her hip bones were prominent and sticking out. She had been through a lot. On her wrists she had rub marks that looked like she had been tied up or chained and then on one of her thighs was the perfect boot print where some fucker had trodden on her.

"What the fuck?" X growled as he took in all her injuries.

"Well she doesn't look like she's been raped, at least not recently, so that is a positive," Doc said as he pointed to her wrists and then her ankles, "however, wherever she came from she had been shackled, they are rub marks, and looking at her right ankle I'd say she wore that shackle for some time."

"Shit," Lolly said as she entered the room, "someone did her bad."

"Do you recognize her?" X asked.

Lolly stepped closer and studied her face, as she bit her bottom lip in concentration and took all the girl in before shaking her head. "No, I haven't seen her before, not around this club anyway. Is she going to be alright?"

"She appears to have a concussion, she has some really nasty cuts to her head, which looks like someone hit her with something heavy. I'll suture her wounds and get her on a drip. She needs fluids, she's dehydrated, and she doesn't look like she has been fed in quite some time," Doc explained.

"Right, well what do you need me to do Doc?" Hadley asked from the doorway.

The room was crowded with bikers and club whores as they all gathered to see if they recognized the girl or could help. This girl was a mystery. Not only as to who she was, but how the fuck she got to the club in the first place. It wasn't like the club was in the metro area. They were right on the outskirts of town. If she walked from somewhere, she would have had to at least cross a major highway to get to where she was found. The fact that she was naked, she surely would have been seen and picked up, someone would have stopped. It didn't matter how shit a town was, if you saw a bruised naked girl roaming the streets, you're going to lend a hand. It didn't make sense as to why she would have come to them, and in her condition, he didn't think she would have successfully walked that far. X knew about adrenalin and the affect it could have on a person, allowing them to manage great feats but he didn't think this was the case.

X looked around the room and chewed on his cheek. His brows furrowed as he tried to think of possible answers. "Who goes out there to smoke usually?" he asked.

Arsen raised his hand, along with Satan, Kyle and Daniel. "Did any of you see a car hanging about or anything out of the ordinary? I don't reckon she walked here, not in this condition," X said.

The men all looked between each other before Kyle's eyes widened, "fuck man, there was a black SUV that drove past real slow when I was out there, that was like two hours ago. I didn't think anything of it, you know what people are like, see a bike club patch and want to slow down to have a look."

X nodded his head; they weren't unaccustomed to tourists that hear about the club and want to drive past to see the big bad bikers. It could have been nothing, but with the appearance of a beaten and naked girl, it made him suspicious. It did mean though that if someone dropped her there, they had to go through the gate that wouldn't be locked yet, but still shut, dump her body before leaving again. Whoever was responsible for dumping this girl here, had some fucking balls.

Blaine came in the room, his face full of fury, his brows pinched and his jaw tight. "I just checked the cameras. She was dumped out of a black SUV an hour ago. The fucking thing had been driving up and down the street all night."

X and Kyle exchanged a look, the SUV that he had seen, obviously was the same car that had dumped the girl. "Did you get a look at the driver? Someone we recognize?" X asked.

Blaine held up a grainy black and white photo that he had obviously printed from the security camera, "he's got a cap on so it's hard to see his face, but look, and tell me what you think? Is it one of the Iron Horsemen?" he asked.

X took the photo from Blaine's hand and looked down at it, studying the guy in a cap that was pulled down low on his forehead, covering the top half of his face. He was obviously aware of the camera's because he did his best to angle his face away from the camera.

"Is this the best shot you've got of him?" X asked.

Blaine nodded his head and sighed, "yeah, he knew the cameras were there, I'd say all his scoping he did allowed him to spot them. So, he was careful about us not to see too much of his face."

X handed the photo over to Satan, who peered down at it and shook his head before passing the photo over to Arsen. The men passed the photo around before handing it to Hadley who growled.

"Fucker," she spat.

X looked up at her with a frown, "that is Pitt Trussard, one of the sons of Gable," Hadley said.

"Are you sure?" Blaine asked taking the photo back from her, "I thought he was dead."

"No, they keep him pretty much locked up, he has disabilities, I'm not sure what, probably from inbreeding, but he is too sweet for this world. Gable hates him, I heard rumors that he feared the kid and doesn't usually let him out of his sight, was it him that was driving?" she asked after explaining more about Pitt.

"He got out of the passenger side, the driver stayed in the car, and I couldn't see who it was driving because of the tint," Blaine replied.

"It would have been Hawk, he is the only one that Gable trusts with Pitt to take him out," Hadley informed them. She was a wealth of knowledge, one of the many reasons that she continued with the club.

"Well, I've done all I can for now, but she is going to need care, I'm not sure how long she is going to be out for, but I'll check her periodically to make sure she is alright," Doc said, standing from where he had knelt beside the bed.

When X looked down at the girl, he noticed, Doc had set her up with an IV in her hand, pumping fluids into her body.

"I've set her up with some antibiotics also, it was lucky I had them on me, actually. Hopefully that will starve off any infection before it becomes a problem. Her head is a fucking mess. I've got pain killers, for when she wakes up. She is going to be in a whole world of hurt with the injuries she has." Doc said before turning to Hadley, "would you mind washing her down and finding some clothes for her?"

Hadley nodded before she turned and left the room to gather water and washcloths.

"Do you mind if I leave her here, I don't want to move her now that I have her situated?" Doc asked looking at X.

"Yeah man, that's fine, I'll crash in one of the guest rooms."

"She doesn't appear to have any broken bones, which is lucky, but she sure is in a bad way. If she is one of the Iron Horsemen, I'm not sure that she is related," Doc explained.

"I didn't think they let outsiders in?" Arsen asked looking down at the girl. His brow was pulled tight into a frown.

"No, I didn't think so either," Doc said with a shake of his head and sigh.

Whoever this girl was, was a mystery. All they knew was that Pitt had dumped her unconscious and beaten body at their door. X could only hope that she would wake up so that he could find out what her story was. This time he wasn't going to allow what happened to Bree happen again. This time if this girl survived, he wasn't going to let her out of his sight.

Chapter Four

Lyric She was swimming in a quagmire of darkness. In the distance Lyric could hear voices but wasn't able to make out anything they said. She tried to cry out to them, she opened her mouth, but her voice wouldn't work. Panic gripped her, moving was like being stuck in quicksand. With every step she tried to take she sunk further. Why couldn't she move? What was this place? She looked around trying to find something in the darkness that could help her. But there was nothing. The place was a void. There was no color, no shapes, nothing, just darkness and those voices that floated through the air occasionally. She couldn't even be sure that they were voices, more sounds, but many different ones.

Lyric stopped fighting and trying to move, she felt her face and the wetness of her tears that were on her cheeks. How did she get to this place? Lyric tried to remember what had happened. She remembered the feel of the cold concrete on her skin, the chains that held her ankles and the rope tight around her wrists, chaffing the skin.

"Please let me go home. My father, he will give you what you need, but please let me go home," Lyric begged.

She didn't know that her father would have whatever it was that the men in front of her needed. She didn't even know what it was that her father owed them. He was just a mechanic who came home every night to look after her and her brothers every day. Ever since her mother died three years previously, he had been their sole provider until her eldest brother Clint was able to help work in the shop. She was the youngest of four. Clint was four years older than her; Brenton was three years older and then

Lachie was two years older. Lyric was only fourteen when her mother died of cancer, there was no warning, one day they went to bed, and the next morning she was dead. Lyric's father explained that she had cancer, but had kept it a secret, so as not to worry her family.

The men that currently had her chained to the wall in an empty concrete room, with no windows had taken her from her home three days earlier. She was at home preparing dinner for her brother's and father when the doorbell rang. She didn't think anything of answering the door. Why would she? Her father and brothers were good men, they wouldn't willingly put her in danger. However, the man with the voice of gravel on the other side of the door, punched her in the face, snapping her head back on her shoulders. Lyric's knees buckled and she crumpled to the floor as she cried out in pain.

"Where are they?" the man growled.

Lyric looked up at him, he had grey hair that was shaved close to his scalp, he looked like he had lived a life of hard work. His muscles weren't from working out in a gym. He wore a leather vest, that had a patch on the front reading president. The man reached forward and snagged her by her hair, Lyric cried out and tears sprung to her eyes with the burning of her scalp.

"I asked you a fucking question," he growled.

Lyric's eyes widened and she shook her head, what could she tell him? "My dad is at work, next door at the shop, Clint is out picking up car parts and is due back today, Brenton and Lachie are at the shop with dad. I don't know what you are looking for," she cried out in panic.

The man raised his hand and she braced herself for the blow that was bound to come, when it connected with her skin, Lyric screamed in pain. She felt her eyebrow split and blood begin to dribble down over her eyes.

"Dad just take her with us, if he wants her back, he will bring them to us," another man spoke from behind the one that held her by the hair.

She looked over at him, his hair was long and shaggy, when he smiled down at her, his teeth were yellowed, and his green eyes watched her with lust. Lyric tried to shake her head, she had to fight, she had to get away from these men. She knew that her dad and brothers would be home soon, if she could fight long enough for them to get home, they would save her. She reached up and dug her nails into the man who held her, she gouged at his arm. He growled and flung his other hand around her throat, squeezing. Lyric felt the air cut from her lungs and her eyes widened with fear. She used all her strength, kicking her legs out, trying to connect with any part of her body. She heard the man grunt when one of her feet connected with him.

The other man wordlessly stepped up and raised his fist. The pain that exploded through her face overwhelmed her and as darkness took over, she felt herself be lifted and carried away from her home, away from her family and away from safety. When she woke, she was lying on a concrete floor, with metal shackles around her ankles and rope tightened against her wrists. Her breathing was coming in short sharp breaths. Her face hurt and she couldn't open one of her eyes. Lyric had been stripped of the clothes she had been wearing and she shivered with the cold.

Movement in the corner of the room took her attention, she glanced over to see a large guy, not much older than her, standing and watching her. Lyric scooted back against the wall. He didn't make any attempt to get closer to her, he just watched her with big eyes. The more she looked at the guy, she realized that he wasn't the same as everyone else.

"Please let me go home. My father, he will give you whatever you need. Please just let me go home," she begged.

The boy cocked his head to the side and took a step towards her. She bit her lip to stop herself from screaming. Her breathing quickened, he continued to step towards her in a lumbering walk. He crouched in front of her and reached out to touch her face. Lyric flinched back and closed her eyes. He stopped before touching her face. When she opened her eyes, she noticed the look of hurt he wore. It was then that she realized that the boy before her, had down syndrome.

"Who are you?" she asked.

"Pitt," he answered.

"How old are you Pitt?"

"I'm seventeen. Are you my girlfriend?" he asked.

Lyric shook her head and sighed, he was a boy. She wondered if he had been taken as well. She didn't even know where she was, or who these people were. Lyric wanted to curl up in a ball and cry, but she couldn't give up. She just hoped that her brother's and father was looking for her.

"I'm not your girlfriend, but I'd like to be your friend, Pitt. My name is Lyric. I'm seventeen as well."

Pitt smiled at her and took one of her hands in his. His hand was huge and enveloped her small hand.

"Friends," he said with a big goofy smile that she couldn't help but return.

The days blended into one another and Lyric soon couldn't remember how long she had been held in that dark concrete box. Pitt was her one constant companion. The man who had taken her, she found out was named Gable, he was the president of a bike club called the Iron Horsemen and according to him, her father had taken something from him. Lyric tried to explain to Gable that her father wasn't a thief, that he was just a simple mechanic trying to make ends meet. But her words fell on deaf ears.

Gable liked to dole out beatings along with one of his sons, Ace. Ace had been the guy who was with Gable when she was taken, and he was even more evil than his father. The way that he watched her, with lust, he terrified her. There was no rhyme nor reason for the beatings that she was inflicted. Some days they wouldn't touch her, and then other days Gable or Ace would come in with their fists flying. The only thing she could be grateful for, was that neither man had attempted to rape her, she always wondered how long it would be before they did rape her, especially Ace.

Chapter Five

X It had been three days since the girl had been dumped out the front of the club house. X called her the girl, because despite their research, they had no idea who she was. Nobody recognized her, she was a complete mystery. Her bruising had started to yellow and the swelling around her eyes eased. X didn't know what was going on with him, but he found he couldn't leave her side. The Doc tended to her during the day but left her in X's care of a nighttime. He would lie on the floor and watch her until sleep stole him. Every morning when he woke, he found himself hoping for something, that she would open her eyes, murmur anything. But three days and still nothing.

Doc said that she was healing well, and being unconscious was the best thing for her, but the seed of worry continued to grow in X's gut. Not knowing who she was, or where she came from unsettled him. X liked control, he liked to have all his i's dotted and all his t's crossed. He didn't have room for chaos, because in his experience, chaos brought trouble. He knew that this girl was going to bring trouble down on him, but he just hoped he could get ahead of it first, so he was the offense rather than the defense. So far all they knew was that at some time she had been with the Iron Horsemen, and it was Pitt and possibly Hawk who dumped her at the Kingsmen's club house.

That was a mystery. From everything that Hadley and Johnny, the two eldest members of the club told them, the fact that Pitt was even allowed out wasn't normal. Pitt was born with down syndrome, Hadley believed it was because of inbreeding. However, Gable, his father, kept him locked up in the club house, the only time he was allowed out was under the supervision of Hawk and then it was only very short outings, to the grocery store for a food run. He was never given free reign. According to Hadley, Pitt was very trusting and talked to everyone, which is why Gable didn't want him to be in public. There was a fear that their secrets would get told if Pitt wasn't controlled.

X tried to think of a way that he could get in contact with Pitt. He had answers about the girl, he must have known her, in a sense he saved her. And it was that, that confused X even more. Why would he save her? Why protect her? There were so many unanswered questions that they made X start to feel physically ill.

"How is she this morning?" Doc asked as he came into the room.

X had not long woken and was sitting watching the girl. She was breathing as normal, her chest rising and falling under the blanket, her eye lids were still closed, and her lips slightly parted with every inhale.

"No changes," he said rubbing his hand over his face, "Doc, what do we do if she doesn't wake up? I mean how long can we expect her to be unconscious for, and what will she be like once she does wake up?"

Doc shook his head and sighed, as he reached over and gave X's shoulder a small squeeze. "Ideally, she would be in a hospital, she would have scans of her brain to tell us the extent of her injuries, but I don't have access to those things here. So, I can't tell you what she is going to be like when she wakes up or when she will wake up. All her vital signs are good, her heart rate is strong, her blood pressure is stable, and she is breathing on her own well. She is hydrated now, and once she wakes, she will start to put on weight. But it's going to be just a waiting game."

"X, maybe we need to take her to the hospital," Hadley said from the door.

She was holding a tub, with soap and a washcloth, Hadley had been washing the girl down every day, keeping her clean and making sure her wounds didn't get infected.

"We can't guarantee she will be safe there, if it was Pitt who dumped her, I can only assume that Gable doesn't know. And for whatever reason, Hawk and Pitt took the opportunity to bring her here, where they knew she would be safe from their father," X said watching as Hadley started to wipe down the girl's hands and arms.

"Is that our problem though? If we take her to the hospital, tell the police what happened, let them keep her safe," Hadley pleaded.

X frowned and shook his head angrily, "No," he growled, "she stays here, for however long it takes, I refuse to take the chance that Gable or any of those other cunts will find her and take her back. I believe the reason Pitt dumped her here was to save her, and if that's the case, then I'm going to save her."

Hadley sighed and nodded her head, resigning to the fact that she wouldn't be able to get X to budge on his opinion. The girl was now under his care, if he had to claim her to do so, then that's what he would do. He wasn't going to take the chance that what happened to Bree would happen to her as well.

Chapter Six

Lyric

Her head felt like she was floating as the darkness around her began to get brighter. The voices that Lyric had been hearing while she was in the darkness, started to get louder.

"Why the hell would Pitt dump her here? Gable mustn't know, he'd never allow that to happen," a deep voice spoke.

Pitt? She remembered Pitt, she remembered Gable. Lyric shuddered at the thought of the damage that Gable did to her. He was cruel beyond anything she could imagine. He had taken her from her father, from her brothers, he insisted that they had something of his, he insisted that she was taken from them to pay for their sins. He beat her senselessly. He said he was training her; she was to become a brood mare. He really did refer to her as animal stock. Lyric wouldn't submit though, she couldn't submit, she knew the minute she did he would rape her, and she be forced to carry the child of this cruel and horrible man.

Pitt though, such a beautiful soul, in a world that was too dark for him. He was treated just as harshly. Gable didn't beat him like he did Lyric. It was almost like Gable was somewhat afraid of Pitt, afraid to push him too hard. So instead he locked him away for days on end, with no food and only a dirty bucket of used water that she had been washed with to drink. Lyric spent hours singing and talking with Pitt. He told her about his dreams, that one day he was going to be a doctor, he was going to help the sick and make people better again. His childlike quality warmed her heart and kept her fighting.

But where was she? Where had Pitt taken her? The darkness began to sink around her again as she thought back to the day before the darkness took over.

"Wake up girl," Gable growled in her ear.

Lyric's eyes shot open and she scuttled back against the wall, Gable sneered down at her in the darkness, his yellow teeth bared in a wolf like snarl. Slowly he shook his head and sighed.

"You are never going to submit, are you?" he growled.

"No," Lyric answered, her voice strong as she snapped the one-word answer.

There were days that she thought it would be better if she did just submit, if she just gave him what he wanted, but she couldn't do it. The beatings were bad enough, but she couldn't imagine how much worse it would be to have to let him have sex with her. She involuntarily shuddered at the thought of it. She was still a virgin, even at seventeen she felt like she was behind the other girls her age. A lot of her friends had already lost their virginity, but she was pleased to hold onto it. Lyric wasn't waiting until marriage, but she didn't want to just throw it away for some boy who would dump her after their first time. So, the thought of Gable taking that piece of her body, filled her with horror.

Gable growled and snagged his fist in her hair, pulling Lyric's face close to his. "Listen bitch, I'm tired of you, I'm tired of your attitude and the way you think you're fucking princess. But I'm here to tell you, that you are fucking nothing, where is your father hmm?"

Lyric frowned and shook her head. She had wondered that. Where was her father or her brothers, surely if they knew where she was, they wouldn't have left her here to rot? Gable seemed to like the look on her face as he chuckled and clicked his tongue.

"Your father gave you to me. I bet you didn't think that was going to happen. I bet you thought he was going to come in here on a shining white horse like some knight and save you from the big bad ogre," Gable laughed, "instead, he said I could keep you as payment."

Lyric shook her head, her eyes widening. Her father would never do that, he called her his little girl, no matter how big she got. He loved her, he always said he would protect her. Gable had to be lying.

"No, that's not true," she growled.

Gable laughed a bellowing laugh as he threw his head back. "Stupid princess bitch," he growled before curling his hand into a fist and slamming it into her cheek bone.

Pain spread through her face and she saw stars begin to float behind her eyes, before the darkness had a chance to fully claim her, Gable took her by the shoulders and slammed her into the wall. Lyric's head ricocheted off the wall, her knees grew weak and she started to lose balance. Darkness crept into the corners of her vision as her eyesight blurred. The last thing she remembered was Gable's fist slamming down into her face again.

Lyric tried to call out to the man's voice that she heard speak. Who was he? And how did he know Pitt and Gable? The floaty feeling in her head started again, it felt like her whole body was starting to drift, her arms and legs became light, as the darkness began to ebb away.

Lyric blinked open her eyes, everything was blurry, and she could hear movement around her. Her breathing began to come out in sharp pants as panic started to take over, she blinked her eyes rapidly, trying to focus on anything to let her know where she was.

"Hey, hey now, come on, you're alright," a gentle woman's voice cooed.

Lyric hadn't seen another woman in her whole time with Gable, maybe she hadn't been hearing things when she heard that Pitt had dumped her somewhere. Lyric blinked again and concentrated on slowing her breathing. Inhaling and exhaling slowly. Her vision started to clear, and she looked up at a weathered red head staring back down at her. The woman's green eyes were filled with compassion and her face was kind. A sob escaped Lyric's lips. She hadn't seen a friendly person other than Pitt in god knows how long. She didn't have any idea of how long she had been held captive by Gable, she knew it would have to have been weeks if not months.

"Come now, sweetheart, you are safe here, no one will touch you," the woman spoke gently, "you just let it all out."

Lyric nodded her head, as forceful sobs spilled from her body, tears trickled down over her face. Could she believe that she was safe? If she was no longer with Gable, then she had to be safe right?

"Where am I?" Lyric asked.

The woman took Lyric's hand in hers and patted it gently, much like a grandmother might, "you are in the club rooms of the Kingsmen. A man named Pitt and we believe his brother Hawk, dumped your body out the front of the club rooms four days ago, do you remember your name?"

She'd been in the darkness for four days, and she was no longer with Gable. Pitt had saved her, but how she didn't know. Lyric knew that he was close to his brother Hawk, he talked about him all the time. Pitt said he hated all his other brothers because they were mean to him, she never saw any of the others, apart from the day that they had taken her from her father's house. However, Pitt loved Hawk and it seemed Hawk was just as fond of Pitt. He would often join them and sneak in a packet of cards. He begged Lyric to give in to Gable, but she couldn't do it.

"My name is Lyric, I'm seventeen years old, I think, I don't know how long I've been gone for," she said.

The lady gave her a warm smile and nodded her head, "my name is Hadley, I've been washing you and caring for you along with Doc, who really is a doctor," she chuckled, "and Maverick, or X as he is known."

Lyric's eyes widened she didn't like the idea that she had been unconscious and vulnerable while a man helped care for her. Hadley seemed to sense her panic and shook her head, squeezing Lyric's hand.

"Only I cleaned you and cared for your hygiene, Doc made sure your wounds were healing and X only made sure no one came after you.

I promise you were safe here; no one took advantage of you and no one will while you are here. Can you tell me how you came to be in Pitt's care?"

Lyric sighed and nodded her head, "Gable, and one of his son's, Ace, took me from my home. Gable said that my father had something of his, so took me as ransom. But then he told me that my father sold me to Gable. He was going to use me as a brood mare he said, because he needed new blood to make the family stronger," she explained shuddering at the thought.

Hadley frowned but nodded her head, "did anyone touch you, I mean, inappropriately, you know, sexually?"

"No," Lyric answered, "he said I had to submit to him before he would bring his sons in, because I wasn't trusted, but I refused to submit. On the day that he knocked me out, he was going to rape me whether I submitted or not, but he punched me, and I fell unconscious."

Hadley hummed in the back of her throat and frowned, "are you a virgin?"

Lyric's eyes widened and panic began to creep into her mind again as she nodded her head. Had something happened to her while she was unconscious, had he raped her after he knocked her out? Suddenly Hadley stood and went to the door, swinging it wide open. On the other side she saw two men standing. One was enormous, he filled almost the entire doorway. He had black hair that hung down over his shoulders, his eyes were the darkest brown she had ever seen, almost black. His muscles showcased the tattoos that ran up and down his arms and creeped out the top of his shirt along his neck. The other man was an older man, with greying hair, he was tall but not as tall as the other, and he was quite slim. He wore dark framed glasses and smiled down at Hadley.

"Doc, can you come in here for a minute please?" Hadley asked.

The older man gave a nod and turned to the other before clearing his throat, "sure thing, just me?"

Hadley nodded, "X can come in soon."

Doc nodded his head and followed Hadley back into the room, while she shut the door, with the man named X on the other side.

"Hi there, you've been through a right rough time, haven't you? I'm glad to see you awake though," Doc said, "I'm Jacob, but everyone calls me Doc. I'm a doctor. I've stitched up the few wounds you had on your face and head, and gave you some fluids, you were very dehydrated."

"Yes, I wasn't allowed to have food or water very often," Lyric explained.

Doc frowned but nodded his head, "I heard what you told Hadley, about where you had been," he said as he turned to Hadley, "what did you need me to check?"

"I want to see if she was raped while she was unconscious. We don't know what happened once Gable knocked her out, so I just want to make sure he didn't assault her that way as well," Hadley explained.

Doc nodded again and sighed, "I'm sorry Lyric, I know that this will be very uncomfortable and awkward for you. I heard you tell Hadley that you were a virgin, which means if you were raped your hymen will no longer be intact. I didn't notice any evidence of sexual assault however, I must admit I wasn't looking for it, as your body was in such damage, that I wanted to get the worst fixed up first."

"What do you need to do?" she asked licking at her dry lips, that were cracked and still a little bit swollen, from obviously being punched.

"I need to check you internally, I will feel for a hymen, it will be very quick, and Hadley will be in the room with you the whole time."

"If my hymen is no longer there? What then?" she asked trying to keep the panic at bay as to what might have happened to her.

"Well unfortunately it will be too early to do a pregnancy test, but I will be able to draw blood to check for STI's and in around four weeks' time, if you are still with us, we can do a pregnancy test, but it takes about four weeks, before a pregnancy will show," Doc explained.

"Everything will be alright, we will make sure you are safe, if you want me to call the police, or your dad or you want us to take you to the hospital then we will do it, you just say the word of what you need and I will make sure it happens," Hadley said, taking Lyric's hand again and giving it a pat.

Lyric nodded and sighed, looking between Doc and Hadley, "okay, let's check," she said.

The test only took a matter of seconds, as much as she was mortified to have Doc's fingers inside her, he was very gentle, and Hadley continued to squeeze Lyric's hand in support. Lyric stared at the roof, too embarrassed to make eye contact with either Doc or Hadley.

"Lyric, you weren't raped, sweetheart, your hymen is still intact," Doc said with a warm smile.

Lyric let out a breath she didn't realize she was holding and felt fresh tears start to fall over her cheeks with relief. Gable may have beat her senselessly, he may have taken her from the only people she loved but he didn't take that one piece of her body that was hers to give, that she had control over. Hadley pulled Lyric into her arms, sitting her up and rocking her back and forth, cooing in her ear, until her sobs subsided.

"Hadley, I'd like to ring my dad please?" she asked.

Hadley looked down at her and smiled, "of course sweetheart, let me get my phone, and you can give him a call."

Chapter Seven

X He paced the hallway while Doc was in there. They had heard Hadley ask Lyric if she was a virgin. Fuck, if she had been raped, he didn't know how he was going to react. Doc opened the door and stepped out. X looked up over at him.

"She is still intact," Doc said, X let out a gush of breath that he hadn't realized he was holding.

He couldn't explain his feelings towards this girl, but even her name Lyric, did something to his soul. She seemed to have grabbed a piece of his heart and he couldn't give her up. X shook his head and ran his hands up over his face, he needed to get a grip. Blaine came down the hallway and looked over at him.

"She's awake?" he asked.

"Yeah, her name is Lyric. She was taken by Gable and held there, she was going to be turned into a fucking baby factory," X spat.

"Shit, so where did she come from?" Blaine asked.

X shrugged his shoulders, "she said that she was taken from her dad's house. She asked Hadley if she could ring her dad, so I guess we will find out soon."

"What a fucking clusterfuck," Blaine said.

"You can say that again."

The bedroom door opened, and Hadley stepped out of the room, her eyes held a sadness he saw when she looked at the other girls that had come through their doors. She was like their club mum, she always kept the girls under her wing, but it seemed Lyric had crept under her skin just as she had X's.

Hadley shook her head and sighed, before nodding down the hallway, leading X and Blaine further into the club rooms. When she stopped just before the bar room doors, she ran her hands up over her hair.

"I don't know what kind of fucked up situation that little girl has found herself in, but it's not a good one," she sighed.

"What do you know?" Blaine asked, folding his arms across his chest.

"I gave her my phone to ring her dad, she used the number she had for him, but it had been disconnected, she tried her three brothers. All three numbers had been disconnected. She even tried to ring the auto shop she said her dad owned, and that number was disconnected. If your little girl has been abducted, why the fuck would you disconnect all your numbers?" she explained.

X frowned, it made no sense, unless what Gable told her was the truth, that her father had given her to him. What kind of fucked up father would do that to his little girl? X just couldn't believe that, that would be the case. Looking over at Blaine's face, X could see that he was thinking the same thing.

"We have her name now, let's get Arsen looking online to see if there was a missing person's report put out for her, that will at least give us a bit more of an idea if she was abducted or sold. How long has she been missing for?" Blaine asked.

"Gable took her on the 15th of December," Hadley answered.

X's eyes widened, it was now July, seven months she had been gone for. He couldn't believe that she had never been raped in all that time, the story wasn't adding up. Gable would fuck his own daughter to procreate, fuck, the rumors said that his sons were byproducts of him fucking his sister's. Gable himself was a created in an incestuous affair between his father and his eldest sister. The whole situation was fucked up.

X, Hadley and Blaine stood silent, lost in their thoughts. X could see that Hadley was worried about her, but Blaine was trying to work out the mystery, while X wondered what this girl was hiding. It was obvious that she hadn't been raped, Doc confirmed that, and he believed she was beaten. But seven months? X shook his head. He just couldn't be sure that she was telling the truth. Had she been planted here? Could Gable be setting the whole thing up, to try and bring the club down from the inside. He ran his hands up over his face. X was exhausted, it had been a long four days. He needed sleep, his mind wasn't clear, and it made it difficult to think about their next steps.

"I'm going to go for a ride past the auto shop, maybe that will give us an idea of what the hell is going on. Some of this story isn't adding up and we are missing too much information," X said, breaking the silence.

Blaine nodded his head and clapped X on the back, "I'm going to come with you, Gannon can hold down the fort, and get Arsen looking into missing persons reports," he said before turning to Hadley, "I want you to keep chatting with Lyric, X is right, something isn't sitting well with me. She was missing too long for her not to have been integrated into Gable's system. She should have already been impregnated by now, the man is a pig, and it's not like him to wait for consent. I want you to see if her story stays the same."

Hadley nodded her head and frowned; her eyes widened as she realized suddenly that what Blaine was saying was true. There was no way that Gable would have waited for Lyric to be ready to willingly have sex with him. If her story was true, there was more that they didn't know. X didn't like not having all the facts, not being in control made him nervous, because where there was no control there was chaos, and chaos meant trouble. Trouble that X didn't have time for.

The ride over to the auto shop took less than ten minutes. If Lyric's father hadn't sold his daughter, it might astonish her to realize just how close by she was held. When they pulled up out the front of the shop, it was easy to see that the place was abandoned. The front windows were boarded up and the place was like a ghost town. X killed the engine on his bike and sat looking at the shell of a building. To the side of the shop was a small weatherboard home. The windows of the house were smashed, and the sides of the walls had been vandalized. X wondered if this was perhaps where Lyric's family had lived.

Blaine stepped off his bike and looked around, "come on, let's go and see what we can find," he said.

X nodded before stepping off his bike and taking his helmet off. He flicked his head towards the house, "I think we should check out the house first," he said.

Blaine nodded and started to make his way over to the home. Once they got to the front door, it was then that X noticed the police tape. "Shit," he swore, this wasn't good. Looking over at Blaine, he saw that he was thinking the same thing as X. If there was police tape across the front of the home, that means something went down, possibly more than an abduction.

Lifting the tape, X climbed under and entered the darkened house. The first thing he noticed was that despite the vandalism that seemed to have happened to the outside of the building, the inside was relatively untouched. Furniture still sat in the places where it was last used, books were neatly stacked in a bookshelf. The television remote tossed carelessly on a coffee table, as if someone just got up from the couch. The only real tell that they were in an abandoned house was the musty smell in the air from having been locked up.

Slowly X and Blaine started to move their way through the house, when they got to the kitchen, they noticed rotting food that was still sitting on a bench, like someone had been making dinner all those months ago. On the center of the kitchen floor, was a large rusty brown stain. X immediately recognized what it was, blood. There was too much blood for just a small injury, this is a stain that had been caused by someone's death.

"X," Blaine called, X looked over his shoulder to see Blaine standing at a door that looked like it could lead into a back yard.

Blaine ran his finger over a series of holes, which X recognized. They were bullet holes caused by a shot gun.

"Shit," X groaned, "There was no evidence Lyric had been shot, so this has to be one of her family members doesn't it?"

"Yeah I reckon so," Blaine confirmed.

They continued to move through the house, when they reached a hallway, they found two more blood stains, one outside a masculine looking bedroom and the other outside a bathroom. Once again there were the same pellet holes scattered over the wall and door behind the stains. Three people at least had been shot in the house. X wasn't sure how many people Lyric had in her family, he knew at least of a father and brothers, but he didn't know if there was a mum and how many brothers. Hadley had told them that all the numbers Lyric tried was disconnected, that means that she hadn't been able to get in contact with any of her family. If Gable had orchestrated the execution of her entire family, it made X believe her story to be true.

Blaine opened a door at the end of a hallway and growled, X followed him down and looked in the room. It was a girl's bedroom; he knew that it was Lyric's room without even having to search. In the middle of her floor, right beside her bed was another blood stain. Four people, one of them having been killed in her bedroom. As they stood looking around, Blaine's phone shrilled out a ring, causing them both to jump and swear.

"Arsen," Blaine barked down the line. Blaine listened as the prospect explained what he had found in his search, his frown getting deeper and his face reddening with anger. When he hung up the phone Blaine turned and shook his head.

"Her entire fucking family was slaughtered. Her eldest brother was found in the kitchen with his head blown off, her two other brothers in the hallway and her father in her bedroom. He got it the worst. He wasn't simply shot. He had been held and tortured over a period of time, before he finally died as a result of his injuries," Blaine explained.

X looked down at the bloodstain in the middle of Lyric's bedroom and shook his head, this kid had been thrown into a world that she should never been a part of.

"Her mum?" X asked.

"Already dead, apparently died when she was younger, they believe the father was running drugs for Gable on the side, the auto shop being the front for the real money."

"Fuck, were the brothers in on it too?" X asked.

Blaine shrugged his shoulders and shook his head, "dunno, Arsen didn't say, he said that he was able to get a hold of the police report. They suspected Gable, but you know as well as I do, what cops we don't have in our pocket, he has in theirs, so I don't imagine anyone would have investigated it too hard."

X ran his hands up over his face, he didn't know what to do or what to even tell the girl. She seemed to have had no idea what extracurricular activities her father was into. It still didn't answer the question as to why Gable had left her intact for as long as he did, and X wasn't sure that he could still trust her. There were more answers to questions he didn't know, but slowly the story was starting to unravel.

Chapter Eight

L yric

Doc was sitting with Lyric when the door swung open and a young blonde guy came into the room. His entire face was pierced, but that wasn't what drew Lyric's eyes, it was the sadness in his eyes.

"Hi, my name is Arsen," he said with a smile, "um, Blaine our Pres and X asked me to come and talk to you to help find your family. I'm kinda good with computers."

Arsen held up a laptop and gave an awkward smile. Lyric nodded her head; she was grateful that they wanted to help her find her dad and her brothers. She tried to ring them, but all the numbers were disconnected, even the shop number. Her stomach churned with the thought that there was a possibility that what Gable said was true, her father had sold her, he didn't want her. That whatever he had taken from Gable meant more to him than his own daughter. She didn't want to believe it, but what alternative was there?

Arsen sat down in a chair beside Lyric's bed and opened his laptop. "Blaine told me when you were taken by Gable, he said that Gable believed your dad had something of his?" he asked.

Lyric nodded her head and cleared her throat, "yeah, he wanted to know where it was, but I didn't know what *it* was, he kept saying that if I didn't tell him where it was, then he would take me and keep me as payment. Then on the day that he beat me unconscious he told me that my dad had decided to sell me to Gable, to become breeding stock."

Arsen frowned and nodded his head, "did your dad do drugs? Sell them? Buy them? Or run them for anyone?"

"What? No," Lyric exclaimed, outraged that anyone could assume her dad would do anything like that, "my dad loved me, he worked hard at the shop to give me and my brother's everything we needed."

"And your mum?" Doc asked quietly from the end of the bed where he sat watching the conversation.

Lyric dropped her face to her lap and sighed, "my mum died when I was twelve, she had cancer," she said quietly.

"I'm sorry, cancer is a dreadful disease," Doc replied, reaching out and giving her ankle a squeeze.

Lyric looked up at Doc and gave him a small smile, nodding her head. Arsen typed on his computer and bit his lip as he read.

"What is your dad and brother's names?" he asked.

"My dad's name is Simon McAvoy and my brother's names are Clint, Brenton and Lachlan," Lyric replied, tears started to prickle at her eyes as she thought of them and the time she had been away. Hadley told her that she had been missing for seven months. Had they been searching for her? Had they missed her or had they simply all moved on with their lives and that is why she couldn't contact them.

Arsen sucked in a breath and quickly stood, snapping his laptop shut, causing Lyric to jump in shock. "Sorry, I, um, I've got to go and ring Blaine," he mumbled as he quickly left the room.

Lyric frowned as she watched the door slam shut behind him, when she looked over at Doc, she noticed the look of concern on his face and the frown that was etched into his brow.

"Lyric, I'm going to go and see what that is all about, I'll get Hadley to make you a sandwich, and have her or one of the girls come and help you have a shower," Doc said as he stood and followed Arsen out the door.

Lyric sighed and ran her hands up over her face, tears stinging her eyes. She wanted to go home, she wanted to be back in her house, she wanted her dad, she wanted her brothers. She even wanted the smell of grease that came with living with a family of mechanics. It felt like it had been years since she saw her family, and even though seven months had been a long time, in the scheme of things, it was really a small blip. Her heart ached though when she thought of the fact that she had missed Christmas, she had missed her eighteenth birthday, her dad's birthday, there was so much that she hadn't been able to celebrate with them and unless someone was able to help her find her family there was going to be so much more that she would miss.

Tears started to trek down over her cheeks as sadness sank into her mind. She was grateful for these people who Pitt had inadvertently introduced her to. They could have dumped her somewhere else, they could have sent her back to Gable, or dumped her, nameless and without an identity while she was unconscious in some sterile hospital but instead, they cared for her and were helping her. She didn't understand why and dreaded to think of what she would owe them for their help. Lyric knew what bike clubs were like, she knew how they treated the girls, who weren't old ladies, she had seen it plenty at the shop when different ones came in for parts or to chat with her dad and brothers.

The door opened and Hadley came in with another lady, this one was so beautiful she was almost angelic, with her blonde hair that haloed around her face and her big blue eyes.

"I have a sandwich and some soup for you, I think maybe start with the soup, because I think it's been a long time since you've had something solid in your stomach," Hadley said, setting a bowl of steaming liquid and a sandwich on the table beside the bed.

"Hello, Lyric, my name is Angel, I'm Blaine's wife," the angelic woman said, how ironic was it that her name was Angel?

"Thank you for letting me stay and looking after me," Lyric said.

Angel gave her a smile and waved her hand, "believe it or not, that's what we do," she said, "when we realized that Pitt dropped you here we knew it was for a reason, and he wanted to protect you, so that's what we did."

Lyric nodded her head and smiled at the thought of Pitt, her protector, sometimes she thought the only reason that Gable hadn't raped her was because he was afraid of Pitt. "He kept me safe, and often sane," Lyric said with another smile.

"I've only met him briefly with Hawk, it's just a shame he has the daddy he has, he is a sweet boy," Angel said wistfully.

The three women sat quietly for a moment, all lost in thought. Lyric wondered if they were thinking of Pitt and Hawk also. Both men had grown to be her friends in that prison. She wished there was a way to protect Pitt. Gable would have known that he was the one to take her away from him and he would have made Pitt pay, she could only hope that he survived anything that Gable did to him. She wanted to save him, she wanted to protect him like he had her, but she didn't even know where the place was that she was kept, so didn't know how to reach him.

Hadley cleared her throat and picked up the bowl of soup, and a spoon before handing it to Lyric, encouraging her to eat. As soon as the hot chicken broth touched Lyric's tongue, she had to force herself to slow down to prevent from gulping it down. She didn't realize how hungry she was until that moment. Lyric moaned in enjoyment as the flavor burst in her mouth.

"I can't say I've ever had my soup sound so good before," Hadley chuckled.

"It's delicious," Lyric said, her face flaming with embarrassment at the noises that she was making.

Once Lyric scooped the last spoon full of soup into her mouth, her stomach was full, and her eyes were drooping with contented sleepiness.

"Let's get you a shower and while you're in there, I'll change the sheets, and get you a fresh shirt and some panties to sleep in, then you can get some more rest. Doc said it's going to take a while before your body is healed, and back to normal, you are going to be tired and probably sore for a while," Angel explained, as she helped Lyric to stand from the bed.

The shower was heavenly, even with the awkwardness of Hadley holding her up. Lyric didn't realize how weak she had become, but just standing was more than she could cope with. Once Hadley finished washing Lyric's hair, careful, not to press too hard on the stitched wound on the back of her head and helped her to wash, she flipped the water off and helped Lyric to dry her body. Just the extra movement was exhausting, so, by the time she got back to the bed, and slipped into the oversized t-shirt and brand-new panties that Angel handed her, she was more than ready for sleep. Her head had no sooner hit the pillow before sleep overcame her and she was enveloped in a peaceful slumber.

Chapter Nine

X When X and Blaine came back from Lyric's home, they sat at the bar with Arsen while he went through everything that he found out. X sighed, this was a mess, this poor kid now had no family, because of his enemies. Gable was fucked up, that was expected when he is the byproduct of his father and sister fucking to make him. X ran his hands up over his face and leaned back on the stool, letting the chatter around him drift away.

"What's the story Blaine?" Angel asked from behind them.

Blaine and X turned around to look at her, she had grown up in the club just like he and Blaine did, she knew how everything worked, but nothing like this had happened to them before. X wasn't sure what Blaine was thinking and how he was going to handle it. Technically they didn't have to do anything for the girl, they could just drop her off at the police station and let her go. She had a place to live, it was full of blood stains and bullet holes, but it would be easy fixed. However, the more X thought about letting her go, the more he wanted to hold onto her. She had gotten right under his skin and he hadn't even spoken to her yet. X shook his head and closed his eyes, shaking the thoughts of a broken girl out of his mind.

"She has no one left. The house was full of blood stains from where her brothers and father died, there are bullet holes in doors and walls. She isn't going to want to go back there, and I don't know if she has money that she can fix the place anyway," Blaine said with a shake of his head.

They might have been big bad bikers, men who in public would never show that they cared, but all the men that had seen Lyric lying there helpless, covered in bruises felt something. Knowing that her whole family had been killed and she had been tortured for what had nothing to do with her, and as far as she knew had nothing to do with her family just made everything worse.

"Shit, what are you thinking about doing?" Angel asked.

Blaine sighed and shook his head, "I don't know, love, we are going to have to tell her. She is eighteen, it's up to her what she wants to do, we can take her to the cops, but you and I both know they aren't going to do anything. Gable is as untouchable as we are."

Angel nodded and bit her lip as she tried to come up with a solution. "Who is going to tell her?"

"I will," X said.

Blaine, Arsen and Angel all looked up at him with wide eyes and their mouth dropping open. He wasn't known as having a heart, that's why he was the executioner, he hated, he was angry and had a chip on his shoulder. He would never usually give a shit about a kid, but she reminded him so much of Bree, that he needed to help her, he needed to do what he failed to do with Bree, he needed to keep Lyric safe.

"Are you sure man?" Blaine asked.

X frowned and nodded his head, sighing, "this girl, I can't explain it, but she has wormed her way in here," he said tapping his chest over his heart.

Blaine frowned but nodded his head, "she's not Bree man, just keep that in mind."

X sighed again nodding, before he turned on his heel and headed for his bedroom. He gave a sharp knock on the door and listened, when he heard Lyric call out to come in, he quietly opened the door and poked his head in.

Lyric smiled sweetly at him when he stepped in and shut the door behind him, "hello," she said.

Her voice had a husky quality to it, she reminded him of a blues singer. X could close his eyes and listen to her talk all day. She was beautiful. He noticed that she had been up and showered, the dark blood that had stained her blonde hair was gone, her eyes looked brighter than they had, she still was painfully thin under the blanket. He noticed for the first time that she was wearing one of his t-shirts, he liked it. He wanted to see it on her all the time, he also had an urge to tear it off her and show her how a man should treat her.

"Hello Lyric," he said clearing his throat. "My name is Maverick, or X, that's what they all call me here anyway. How are you feeling?"

She smiled at him again and fingered the ends of her blonde hair, "I'm doing alright, just sore and a bit sleepy. Did you find my dad?"

X sighed and moved further into the room to sit on the chair that was beside her bed. He looked down at his hands, before looking up at her. His face must have said everything, as her eyes widened, and tears welled up in her eyes.

"I'm sorry, we went to the house and the shop. Arsen, investigated the police records, unfortunately your father and brothers were killed, the night that you were taken," X said sadly.

Lyric nodded her head, before a huge sob bubbled from her chest and fell from her lips. Tears started to streak down her face and sobs fell from her mouth, her whole-body shuddering under the weight of her pain. X didn't think, he reached out and took her in his arms, pulling her into his lap. Lyric buried her face into his chest. X rubbed her back and rocked her back and forth, holding her tight to him while she cried. He kissed the top of her hair.

They sat for an hour or two while she continued to sob, eventually he looked down and noticed that Lyric had fallen asleep. He gently slid her back into the bed and pulled the blanket up to her chest. As X went to move away, she started to sob again, in her sleep. X pulled his boots and jeans off, before sliding in beside her. He wrapped her up in his arms, and her tears eased. He lay there allowing sleep to take over him, with a pretty girl in his arms. Something he hadn't done since Bree.

X didn't know how long they had been asleep for, but he woke up to tender fingers running over his face. He cracked his eyes to see Lyric looking down at him and touching his cheek.

"I'm sorry I fell asleep on you," she whispered.

X gave her a small smile and gently squeezed her to his side, "it's alright, I needed a nap it seems anyway," he chuckled.

Lyric giggled and nodded her head, "I haven't slept so soundly ever since Gable took me," she said her voice hitching at the end.

X gently ran his fingers through her hair, careful to avoid the wounds at the back of her head. "What do you want to do now?" he asked.

Lyric shrugged a slim shoulder and sighed, "I don't know what I can do. Is the house bad?"

X grimaced and nodded his head, "yeah, it's going to need some new plaster, and some new flooring," he said.

Lyric sighed and nodded, "I don't have any money, so, I couldn't fix it anyway. I guess I can go to a shelter or something."

"No, you don't need to do that, you can stay here for as long as you need. I think we contact one of the cops that we are friends with, at least if he knows your alive, there might be more that can be done for you," X said.

"Maybe, I don't know if my dad had a will or anything. Not that I care if the house falls down or whatever, but I would like to be able to get some of my mum's things," she said.

"I'll get dressed and get Blaine and Gannon and then we can contact, Steve, he is a detective, he should be able to tell us what is going on with the investigation and what we can do from here on out," X said, standing from the bed, and slipping his jeans back on.

When he turned back to Lyric, he noticed she was blushing, like she had been checking him out, it caused X to smirk. "I'll be back in a minute," he said as he went out to the main bar to find Blaine and hopefully Gannon.

When he came out into the bar, he noticed most of the guys were there, playing pool and drinking. Hadley was running around cleaning up, Johnny was pouring whiskey and beers, while Angel he could see through the window into the kitchen was cooking. X went to the bar and sat in the stool next to Blaine.

"How is she?" he asked looking over at X.

"Yeah, she didn't take the news really well, she fell asleep sobbing."

"Poor kid," Gannon said with a shake of his head.

Gannon was older than Blaine and X, while X's dad and Blaine's dad had been killed, Gannon had managed to escape only being shot in the shoulder. He was big and scary looking. One side of his face was a melted scar, that he got when he was five years old and his mum threw boiling water over him as punishment. X's grandfather shot her in the face while Gannon's dad was in the hospital trying to save his son.

"I think we need to contact Steve, there has to be something he can do for her, if her dad had a will, what happens with the house and the shop," X said looking between Blaine and Gannon.

"Yeah," he said turning to Arsen who was playing pool, "Arsen, come here."

Arsen came to where they were sitting, "did you find a missing report for Lyric?" Blaine asked.

Arsen nodded his head, "it was a part of the report for the murder, they said that there was a daughter that they believed to be missing, but that's all I found."

X frowned, were they even looking for Lyric or did they just assume that she was taken by Gable and give up. "Who was the detective on the case?" X asked.

Arsen frowned and pulled his phone out of his pocket, pulling up the reports and reading through them, "it was James Burton," he said.

Blaine, Gannon and X all groaned, "well that explains why they didn't look too hard for the kid," Gannon said with a sigh.

"Yep," Blaine agreed.

"What do you mean?" Arsen asked.

"Burton is on Gable's payroll," X answered.

"Shit," Arsen groaned as he realized the problem, "that's definitely why they didn't bother looking for her, that's fucked. I mean I know we do shit that isn't legal, but kidnapping? That's fucked."

"Kidnapping, with the intent to fucking rape her and turn her into some baby factory for Gable's fucked up needs," Blaine growled.

X clenched his teeth and shook his head. He already held nothing but hatred for Gable and the whole of the Iron Horsemen, but this situation made him want to go in and burn the place down with all the club members inside.

"I wonder why Pitt saved her then?" Arsen asked.

"That's a question that I keep asking, X find out what her relationship was like with Pitt and Hawk. Doc said she was still a virgin, so it wasn't a sexual relationship, but for Pitt to defy his dad like that, something doesn't sit right with me," Blaine said.

X nodded and stood up stretching, he had a few questions that he wanted to ask Lyric, the most important one being how it came that Pitt chose to save her.

Chapter Ten

Lyric
After X left the room, she lay staring at the ceiling. Her father and brothers were dead. Gable lied to her, not that she was surprised by that. He was willing to beat her and wanted to use her as a brood mare, of course he was willing to lie to her. But she couldn't understand why he waited so long. He had her there for seven months, and according to X, killed her dad and her brothers on the day that he took her, so why wait seven months before even attempting to rape her. Not that she was complaining, the idea of having him inside her body made nausea overwhelm her. However, it didn't make any sense. This was a man who killed as often as he brushed his teeth, rape wasn't any different, and she wouldn't believe for a minute that it was because he had a conscience. All that bullshit he would spew about her being a willing participant, was just that, bullshit.

The door opened quietly, and Lyric looked over, her body was still healing and because she was still malnourished, she couldn't walk very well or even sit for long periods of time without becoming exhausted. X came back in the room with another man, who was dressed in a cheap looking suit. His black hair was plastered to his head with sweat and his glasses slid down the end of his nose.

"Lyric, this is Steve, he is a detective and has worked on the case investigating your dad and brothers' deaths," X said gently.

Steve stepped forward with a smile and jutted out his fat hand at her, Lyric took it gingerly in hers and gave it a quick shake. Steve sat in the chair beside the bed with a sigh and looked over at her.

"I'm really sorry for what happened to you Lyric and for what you have lost," Steve began, "can you tell me what happened the night you were taken?"

Lyric nodded her head and began to go over the story with him, how she was cooking dinner when there was a knock at the door, then the two men, Gable and one of his son's came in looking for whatever her father had supposedly taken from him.

"I know this is going to be a tough question to ask, but your dad or brothers did they ever sell drugs, or even take long trips somewhere?" Steve asked.

Lyric chewed on her lip. She had never seen drugs in the house or the shop before, she would have never thought it possible, but there had to be a reason why Gable killed them, there had to be a reason why he took her. She frowned, thinking back of the random times her brothers or her dad would disappear for a week at a time, they told her it was to get parts they couldn't get sent to them, but now she wondered. When she looked up at X and Steve, they both were watching her, but their faces said they knew the realization she had just come to.

Nodding her head, Lyric sighed, "I never saw them with any drugs, but they would on different occasions have to leave for a few days to a week. They always told me it was to get parts that they couldn't get shipped to the shop. I just believed them, but they were lying to me, weren't they?" she said as tears began to run down over her cheeks.

Steve sighed and nodded his head, "it seems that way. We didn't see any evidence of drug use or dealing when we looked at the shop or the house, was there somewhere that they would have hidden stuff like that?"

Lyric frowned, as far as she knew the only place that her father kept anything important was in the safe that was in the shop. "The safe, how did you get into it?" she asked.

Steve frowned and looked down at his notes, flipping through a few pages before shaking his head, "we didn't find any evidence of a safe there," he said.

"It was in the basement of the shop, it's not hidden or anything," she said.

X and Steve looked at each other before looking back to her, "would you feel up to coming and showing us?"

Lyric sat up and nodded her head, she was nervous about having to go back to the shop and the house, but she wanted to help, she hoped that there would be evidence that would show that Gable was responsible for her family's death and that way the police would be able to arrest him. She suddenly frowned, if she was found and they knew that Gable took her, why weren't they arresting him?

She asked Steve exactly that, he quickly flicked a look over at X before sighing. X sat down on the edge of the bed and took her hand in his, considering his size and how mean he looked, he was so gentle with her.

"Lyric, the thing is, that Gable owns a bike club just like us, they have a heap of the cops in town on their payroll just as we do. So that means that none of the local cops will investigate them, not without their being problems and fallbacks," X explained.

Lyric frowned, before she looked up at Steve and then at X. "How many cops do you have on your payroll in comparison to Gable?" she asked.

"We have slightly more," X answered.

"Then it is in your favor, Steve, surely you can do something can't you?"

Steve blustered before nodding his head and sighing, "I will do what I can," he said.

Lyric knew the lie straight away, she didn't know whether he was just trying to make her calm and tell her what she wanted to hear because he couldn't arrest Gable, or whether he was playing the double agent and was on both Gable and X's payroll. But she decided to leave it for the time being. She would take them back to the shop and hopefully she would be able to find the evidence that they needed, one way or another, she would have answers.

X called Hadley and Angel to come and help her dress. Both the women protested about Lyric going with Steve, X, Blaine and a guy she hadn't met, Gannon, but their complaints fell on deaf ears. Doc said that she would be alright to travel, most of her bruising was now nothing but a greenish yellow hue on her face and apart from the cuts that still had stitches she was physically alright. Lyric still got tired easily from seven months of rarely being fed, and only having limited amounts of water as well as being chained to a wall. It was going to take a long time for her to rebuild the muscle mass that she lost due to her imprisonment, but she knew with time she would heal and get better.

As Lyric stepped outside of the club house she blinked at the bright sunlight. It had been seven months since she saw the sun. When she was younger, she would spend her summer holidays outside all day, her tan was natural, and her hair would brighten to an even lighter blonde. Now, she was pale, and the bright daylight hurt her eyes. The sun warming her skin felt like it was going to burn her, she didn't enjoy the outdoors and freedom that it once brought her. It felt like everything before Gable was now diminished and the bright colors that surrounded her were now dulled, by her pain and what she had been through for the last seven months.

When X led her by her arm out to a black SUV, there was a tall greying man standing by the driver's side. He gave her a warm smile, that reminded her of her dad. She felt an instant pang of sadness at the memory of everything she lost, what felt like forever ago.

"Hello Lyric, we haven't met yet, my name is Gannon. I'm the VP of the Kingsmen," he said with another smile.

She returned his smile, "hello, nice to meet you," she said.

Gannon nodded his head briefly, "I wish it were just under better circumstances," he replied as he climbed behind the wheel of the car.

She couldn't agree more. Everyone at the club had treated her with respect and kindness, she didn't know if this was how they acted around everyone or whether she was getting special treatment. Something told her that this was out of the ordinary, these men weren't usually so loving and kind to complete strangers. X assisted her into the car, and they started off down the road towards the only home she had ever known and the auto shop that her father had inherited from his father and her brothers were supposed to inherit from him. She assumed it was hers now, not that she knew the first thing about cars. Her father was misogynistic, girls were supposed to be cooks and cleaners, they were meant to raise the children, it was the man's job to go out and earn the money.

Lyric sighed at the thought. She was in school, finishing her last year of high school. She had secretly sent off college applications in hopes that her grades would be good enough to allow her entrance to somewhere decent. She had dreams of being far enough away that she felt the thrill of freedom and independence but close enough that she could still come home. She had dreams of being a teacher, giving the same love to students that many of her teachers had shown her. Now though, all that seemed to be lost and forgotten. She never had the opportunity to graduate from high school, any college applications that were accepted would be long lost now. She sighed and watched the world go by, suddenly sitting up straight as she recognized the streets that they drove down and the town they drove through.

Lyric turned to X with a frown. "What town is this?" she asked.

"Peachton," X replied.

Lyric shook her head, "how far from you is Gable's club house or whatever it was that I was kept in?"

"Just on the other side of the town," Gannon told her looking in the rear vision mirror, making eye contact with Lyric.

Lyric ground her teeth together feeling anger rise in her. She had been kept in her town, not ten minutes from her home, for the last seven months. No one was looking for her, because her family was dead, but that didn't explain the cops. They had to have known that she was missing.

"Was anyone looking for me?" she asked, her eyes filling with angry tears.

X sighed and reached out taking her hand in his, "the cops should have been looking for you, but the investigator in charge of the case, is in the pocket of Gable, so he would have swept it all under the rug, with some excuse of a drug deal gone bad."

Lyric growled and her shoulders tensed. She wanted Gable dead, she wanted revenge not just for her treatment, but for Pitt's, for her brothers, for her father. She couldn't explain what her dad had done to be on Gable's radar, but he never deserved to die. Her brothers didn't deserve early death and she sure as hell had nothing to do with any of whatever Gable had going on.

"Did you ever see Gable before he took you, Lyric?" Blaine asked from the front passenger seat.

Lyric chewed on her bottom lip, trying to think whether there was ever a time that maybe he had been at the shop, she remembers there being bikers at the shop regularly, but she never took much notice of them. It was an auto shop; it was expected that there would be people she didn't know there during the day. Lyric shook her head and sighed.

"There were bikers there regularly, but I don't ever remember Gable. I never took much notice of the people at the shop, mainly because my dad didn't want me to have anything to do with the business. I'm starting to wonder if that had anything to do with the fact that dad and Gable were in business together or whatever they were doing," she said with a sigh.

She needed to find answers, there had to be something that could tell her what it was her father was up to. And if the cops hadn't found the safe, maybe that would be where the answers laid.

Chapter Eleven

X watched Lyric's face as they pulled up to the auto shop. Her eyes were welled with tears and he could almost see her panic wafting off her in waves. His heart was shattering for her. He had spent so many years, after Bree was killed, walling himself off, vowing to never let anyone other than his brothers in again, and here this girl was shattering through the walls like she was swinging a wrecking ball. Every time he looked at her, she took his breath away. He wanted to wrap her up in his arms and never let her go, never let her see the horrible evils that this world consisted of.

He had watched her face break when she came to the realization that she had been held only minutes from her home, that Gable wasn't some far away bike club, but was just around the corner. He saw the moment she started to question everything she knew about her father and her brothers. X wanted to save her from that pain and the realization that maybe her father and brothers weren't the innocent men she thought they were. Lyric took a deep shuddering breath as Steve opened the back door to assist her out of the car.

X wanted to growl and snatch her out of Steve's arms, but he had to reign himself in, now wasn't the time to throw dominance around. She needed them to protect her, she leaned on all of them to get her through what she was about to do, and that was to unlock potential answers to who her family really was. With another sigh she started to walk towards the door of the shop, she stopped and leaned down beside the door and lifted the corner of a board from the wall, reaching in she pulled out a key.

Lyric unlocked the door and with another sigh, entered the building with them all following behind her. When he and Blaine had come, they weren't able to get into the shop, and never thought to ask if there was a spare key to the place. X looked around after his eyes adjusted to the darkness of the shop, the place was exactly as it was left, tools, scattered on a bench, a car up on a hoist, the smell of grease in the air. Lyric stopped in the center of the shop and looked around with her hands on her hips, before she turned to Steve.

"Did the police even come in here? This looks like, dad and my brothers just left for the day," she said before pointing at the car that was up on the hoists, "that is my dad's car."

Steve turned to look at X with a frown on his face, "I think we need to get the car down, it might hold some evidence that could be useful, was this the car he took out of town when they went on trips?" he asked looking back at Lyric.

Lyric shook her head, "no, they always took the mustang, if it's still here it will be in the garage at the back of the block," she said pointing towards where X had noticed a garage that seemed to be locked up when he was there last.

"Did they use the mustang any other time?" Steve asked.

Lyric shrugged her slender shoulders, "sometimes, but not often, it was the car that dad said they only pulled out for long hauls because it drove better."

"It seems like an odd car to pick up car parts in," Gannon said quietly.

Lyric looked over her shoulder and shrugged, "I guess you're right, I never second guessed them before, but there had to be a reason they were killed," she said without any emotion in her voice.

X was worried that she was beginning to shut down. He didn't know that this was a good idea and needed to wrap it up, he made eye contact with Blaine who seemed to understand his look.

"Lyric, if you show us where the safe is and open it up, then we will get you back to the club house so you can rest," Blaine said.

Lyric shrugged her shoulders, before nodding again. Her eyes when she looked over at Blaine, looked dead, the shadows were dark, and her face was pale. X moved forward and took her in his arms, "come on sweetheart, you can do this," he said quietly into her hair.

Lyric let out a little sob and shook her head, "I don't know that I can, X, I don't think I'm strong enough to know the answers, I don't think I can take the heart break that my dad and brothers were working with Gable," she sobbed.

X took her arms in his hands and held her back, bending slightly to look down in her eyes, "you can, and you will. We are all going to be right beside you, we aren't going anywhere, you have a home with us, you have a family in us. Is it ideal? No, of course in an ideal world your dad and brothers would still be alive, but you were strong enough to fight against Gable for seven months, you can push through this little bit," he said firmly.

Lyric looked up at him with sad eyes. A look that just about brought him to his knees. This beautiful broken girl was lost. He knew that feeling, he felt the same way when Bree was killed, he felt the same way when his dad died. But like he had the guys to help prop him up, Lyric too, had them, she had him. And he wasn't going to let her go. She seemed to be able to understand the resolute look that he gave her and nodded her head, sucking in a deep breath, before slowly exhaling, raising her shoulders up and turning to head in the direction of what X assumed was the safe.

She led them further into the shop, into what seemed like an office, on one wall was a high shelf filled with auto parts in boxes. Lyric pushed on the shelf, moving it to the side, when it moved out of the way, there was a door. X looked over at Blaine, who frowned, Steve caught X's eyes. They all had the same questions, why would a simple mechanic need a secret door? Lyric flipped the light switch, but the power had been turned off.

"Here, use this, sweetheart," Gannon said reaching out and handing her his phone with the torch light lit up.

Lyric gave him a small smile and pointed the light toward the stairs, before turning to look over her shoulder, "be careful these steps aren't exactly stable, I wasn't allowed down here often, but when I did the stairs were always a bit scary to walk on."

X realized that she was trying to stall them walking down there. "Lyric?" he said drawing her attention to him, "if you want, we can go down there, just write the safe number down, you don't have to do this."

Lyric sighed and dropped her head down on her shoulders, before looking back at them. No one moved, waiting to hear what she would do. Lyric shook her head and turned back towards the steps, "I'm just frightened, what if everything you say, and Gable said is true? What if my dad was a bad man?" she asked, her bottom lip trembled, and her chin wobbled as her eyes welled with tears.

X reached out and took her into his arms, pulling her into his chest and kissing the top of her head. "You might find that everything that has been said is true, and if that is the case, it will hurt, it will fucking hurt so bad, but we are all here. Lyric I'm here, I'm not going anywhere, you've opened up a hole in the wall that I built around my heart, and I'm not going to let you walk the journey on your own anymore."

Lyric sniffed and looked up at him, her big blue eyes filled with tears, but the shadows that he had seen in them since she had woken, seemed to be dissipating. She gave him a small smile and nodded her head.

"I can do this," she whispered.

X bent his head down and kissed her on the corner of her mouth, "you can do this," he said, giving her waist a small squeeze.

Lyric took a deep breath and turned back towards the door that led to the basement and started down the steps. They followed her down, no one said a word. When they got into the basement and saw that it was a giant room with a concrete floor, there was small windows that let a little bit of light in. X looked around, there was a chair that was in the center of the room, one wall was covered in an array of tools, that X recognized. These weren't here to be used on cars or building, these were tools that were used for torture. He knew that if he looked closely, he would find stains of blood on the blades.

Steve was looking over at the wall with a frown on his face, he groaned and shook his head. They all knew what this meant. Lyric's father was into some shit that he kept secret from her, and X would bet that he was working a lot more with Gable than they thought. Lyric was at the safe. She swung the door open and then gasped, before spinning around. X went towards the safe and looked over her shoulder, before groaning.

"Fuck," he spat.

The safe was filled with not only bags of drugs and weapons of all sorts, but in a glass jar, was a head. A fucking head. Nausea washed over X as he pulled Lyric away so she couldn't see. His swearing caught Blaine, Gannon and Steve's attention and they filled the doorway to the safe.

"Fucking hell," Steve said, turning away from the safe and shuddering.

His face was paled in the beam of sunlight that filled the room. Blaine and Gannon shared a look with each other, and X. Lyric had her head buried in his chest, her whole body was trembling. When she looked up at X her eyes were filled with tears, she shook her head.

"Why?" she cried.

"I don't know sweetheart, I know that this is a hard question to answer, but do you know who that was?" X asked, as he ran his hands up and down her back.

Lyric nodded her head and a sob fell from her lips, "my mum," she cried, as she clasped his shirt in her fists.

"What the fuck?" X growled.

Lyric shook her head, "he said she had cancer, she was supposed to have died of cancer, why, why the fuck would he do that? What sick piece of shit does that?" she said hysterically, her voice rising as her panic started to take over.

X held her tight against his chest and turned to lead her up the stairs, she didn't need to be in the room. Her fucking mother's head was in a safe, in a fucking glass jar. What the fuck kind of man does that? X's head was spinning. How did this girl not know what he was doing? She sobbed the whole way up the stairs, her whole body was shaking.

"X, who was my father?" she said just above a whisper.

X just shook his head; he didn't know how to answer her. He didn't know who the man was and how the hell any man could do that. He just hoped that Steve would be able to investigate it further and get some answers for Lyric.

When they got out into the yard, Lyric's sobs had turned into sniffles, her face was tear stained and red. "I thought I would be more upset, but I don't know, I think maybe I knew that he wasn't the man I thought he was," she said quietly.

"Why do you say that?" X asked.

Lyric shrugged her shoulder, "I can't say for sure, but I feel like I had a gut feeling, like I already knew I was going to find something horrible in that safe. That the answers that I was going to get weren't going to be good. I mean, everything sort of just points to it didn't it? The bikers that were always here, the weeklong trips in the mustang, me not being allowed to go down to the basement, the secrets, and when I came into a room, how my brothers and dad would stop talking. I was just too stupid to see it, I just accepted everything they told me."

Lyric's sobs started again, X continued to hold her and soothe her, rubbing his hands up and down her back. He didn't know whether it wasn't hitting her yet, or she was truly just numb to everything. He had expected her to react far worse, especially seeing her fucking mothers head in a jar. X couldn't get past that, who the fuck does that? Steve came out of the building and towards X, he was wearing a frown and X knew that he was going to investigate everything further.

"Lyric?" Steve called, drawing Lyric's attention to him, "I'm going to get a team here to start investigating everything, but when your mum died, you said, that you believed she died of cancer? Where was she buried?"

Lyric looked up at him and then off in the distance, "we had a funeral for her, here, it was only my dad, brothers and I, we were the only family she had. Dad and my brothers dug a big hole and made a coffin for her."

"Can you show me where? I don't mean to be crass, but we might have to remove her body in order to investigate further whether she had cancer or if she was murdered," Steve said.

Lyric's head snapped to him and her eyes widened like it hadn't occurred to her that there was a possibility that she had been murdered. X could see that Steve was regretting what he said, but how could he have made it better? How do you nicely tell someone that their father might have murdered their fucking mother? Lyric sighed and nodded her head, before she started walking towards the back of the property.

"My grandfather and grandmother are buried back here too," she said quietly.

X held Lyric's hand as they walked, behind the big garage, that must be the one that held the mustang was three head stones. Lyric led them until they stood in front of her mother's. The head stone was a simple wooden cross with the name, Emily Louise McAvoy, etched into it.

"This is my mum, then that's my grandfather and grandmother," she said quietly, looking over at the other two head stones, that were also just simple crosses, one read James John McAvoy and the other Violet Grace McAvoy.

"So, these were your father's parents?" Steve asked.

Lyric nodded her head. "Where were your mother's parents?" Steve asked.

Lyric shrugged her shoulder and shook her head, "I don't know, they never talked about them," she said quietly, "I never asked."

Lyric gave a humorless laugh before shaking her head, "I think I should have asked a lot more questions," she said bitterly.

Steve reached out and gave her shoulder a small squeeze, "I'm sorry Lyric, but we will get to the bottom of it all, we will work out what was going on here," he said to her.

Lyric looked up at him, her eyes, that had started to shine before they went into the basement were now dead again as she nodded her head at him. "I'm not sure that I want all the answers," she replied.

"I will only tell you as much as you want," Steve assured her.

Lyric nodded again and sighed. "Where do we go from here? I don't even know where my dad and brothers' bodies are. I don't know what I do about this place, I don't have any other family, so where am I supposed to go? What do I do?"

The panic that she had in her voice when they were in the basement was starting to bleed through. X took her in his arms again and looked down at her, making eye contact. "You have a place to go, you stay with me for as long as you need to, as for this place we will work out with a lawyer what needs to happen. Your dad and brother's bodies we will find. You aren't alone in this, you've got me, you've got all of us, and now you have Steve on your side, you aren't alone."

Lyric nodded and wrapped her arms around his waist, pulling herself tight against him. She breathed in and rested her head on his chest. X kissed the top of her head and held her tight.

Chapter Twelve

L yric

She was numb, everything inside her felt dead. Lyric knew she shouldn't feel that way, she should be angry, grief stricken, vomiting, screaming, anything, but dead. Her mind was filled with questions that seemed to have no answers. What could she tell them? That she had been so caught up in herself that she hadn't noticed what was going on right under her nose. Her father had her fucking mother's head in a fucking glass jar. Who the fuck does that? What kind of man was he? And did her brothers know or were they just as unaware as she was?

Lyric searched through memories, anything, that would tell her that underneath everything she knew, she knew that her dad was nothing but scum. Instead she continued to come up blank. Other than the fact that there were bikers regularly at the shop, there was nothing that connected him to Gable. However, even if she had known, what could she have done about it? There was nothing she could do, she had no where she could run to, she was trapped, her father controlled her every move. Lyric always thought that was because he was overprotective, that he didn't want her to make stupid choices, but now she wondered what the motive behind his every word and action was.

Her, X and Steve stood staring down at the grave that she thought held her mother, but did it really? Apparently, it didn't hold her fucking head. Tears continued to stream down her cheeks, she didn't know what to do or even how to do it anymore. X said that she was strong enough, but she wasn't, she wasn't strong, she was just good at pretending, over the last seven months she had become good at pretending, that was all.

"Lyric? Is the garage where the mustang was kept locked up?" Steve asked.

Lyric looked over her shoulder at the shed, and sighed, she wondered what horrors they would find in there, she nodded and started towards the garage. X slipped his hand into hers and held her as they walked. It felt good being so close to him, it felt like she could draw on his strength. Over the last seven months she had turned off any semblance of hormones that she could have possibly had, but whenever she looked at X, she couldn't help the butterflies that floated around her belly. He was obscenely good looking, like grace the cover of a magazine good looking. When he held her eye contact, she got lost in his eyes, when he pressed her against him, she could feel every hard plain of his body. A body that she would like to explore further.

Lyric shook her head, now wasn't the time to think about such things. X squeezed her hand and when she looked up at him, he was watching her with a small frown. If only he knew that she had been thinking of climbing him like a tree. Once they got to the doors of the garage, she reached into the pocket of the wall to find the key. Unlocking the door, she swung it open and entered, the garage was still the same, the only thing in the whole place was the mustang, under a large sheet. Lyric rolled up the big door to bring in light. When Steve tried the doors to the mustang, she realized it was locked. Lyric frowned.

"The keys would have been in the house, on his bedside table, it's where dad kept them," she said quietly.

X and Steve exchanged a look that she didn't understand, before Steve suggested he would go and find the keys. She wasn't sure if she wanted to go into the house, unlike the shop and the garage, the house held all her memories, it was where, other than school, she spent all her time, it's where her mother's things were. Lyric wasn't sure she would be able to see those and not break. She preferred the numbing sensation that had taken over, and she wasn't sure she was ready to deal with the pain that came with seeing and touching the memories of her life before Gable.

"How are you holding up?" X asked quietly as he took Lyric in his arms.

Lyric looked up at him, he had the darkest hair she had ever seen and eyes so dark they were almost black. She shrugged her slender shoulder and sighed. "I don't know, I don't know how I feel. I'm hurt, angry," she said before shaking her head, "no, not angry, I feel red hot rage, I feel betrayed, I feel like everything my father told me was nothing but a lie."

"Baby, look at me," X said touching two fingers under her chin and lifting her face so he could look into her eyes, "you are right to feel everything you are feeling, and we will find the answers, and I assure you that you will have your revenge."

"To who?" she asked.

X smirked and kissed her lips gently, just a small peck, but it sent a flutter of butterflies through her stomach, "to Gable."

Lyric smiled up at him, she wanted that revenge. Her dad, well she had no words for whatever the hell that was, and she knew that Steve was planning on investigating and he would discover what was needed, but she wanted revenge against the man who had held her captive for seven months. The man who had beaten, starved and threatened to breed her. She wanted his body carved up and his head in her own jar. Its scared Lyric that she was so quick to think those thoughts, she had always abhorred violence, but after spending months at the hands of that man, and then to discover that her life had been a lie, violence seemed like the better option. To no longer be on the defense but to be the offense.

Movement at the door drew Lyric and X's attention, and when she looked over, she saw Steve come back in holding up a set of keys with a pensive frown etched into his brow. He clicked the button on the remote and the car beeped, unlocking the doors. Steve opened the door of the driver's side and popped the trunk. Lyric groaned at the sight that was there, nausea swept over her and vomit started to purge up her throat. Lyric ran from the garage, making it just outside the door before hot vomit was splashing down at her feet. She felt X's hands pull her hair back off her neck and rub her back until she had nothing left to bring up, not that she had a lot to empty in the first place.

"What the fuck?" Blaine shouted, he and Gannon had come into the garage just as Lyric ran from the room to vomit.

She couldn't believe what she had seen. A humorless laugh bubbled from her body, until she was cackling like a woman gone mad, and maybe that was it, she had finally lost the plot. How the hell could she have felt so numb at seeing the head of her own mother in a jar, kept by her father, yet the bodies of naked rotting corpses was what tipped her over the edge. Lyric's laughter soon turned into wracking sobs that shook her entire system. Her knees buckled underneath her and if it weren't for X's quick reflexes she would have collapsed into her vomit.

X held her tight against him, while she sobbed, asking God or any entity why? Why her? Why her family? What had she done so wrong that she should be subjected to this? It didn't take long for exhaustion to take over her system and her mind to collapse into darkness as sleep took over in the safety of X's arms. A man she had literally known for a day, a man that she trusted more than the family she had grown up with. A man that she believed when he said would keep her safe.

Chapter Thirteen

X This was fucked, this whole place was fucked, someone needed to take a match to it and light the fucker on fire. This poor beautiful girl, to find out that her father was, fucking whatever, X didn't even have words to describe him, to see her mother's head in a fucking jar. Who the fuck does that? He couldn't believe what he had seen when Steve popped the trunk of the mustang. At least three dead bodies, from what he could tell they were female, but X couldn't be sure, they were rotten, just beyond stinking, but unrecognizable. Obviously, they had been in the trunk when Lyric was taken, and her father and brothers killed. X just hoped they were already dead, the thought of them being alive and suffering until death finally took them, it caused nausea to well up and his eyes to water.

"Steve, we need fucking answers to this, I don't know what kind of fucked up house of fucking horrors this is, but we need answers. Obviously, Gable is involved, he wouldn't have taken Lyric and killed her family if he wasn't," X said.

Steve just nodded his head, his face was pale as he stared at the trunk of the car, like he was unable to grasp what the hell was going on. That made two of them.

"Yeah, yeah, I'll, um, I'm going to call it in," Steve answered with a shake of his head.

Blaine was on the phone to their prospects Arsen and Hale organizing for them to come and collect Lyric's belongings from her room, while Gannon was inside the house searching for anything that might give them some answers that the cops missed the first time. X gently placed Lyric in the back of the SUV, she had fallen asleep in his arms after sobbing. This was too much for her, and they should never have brought her back here, but without her they wouldn't have been able to get into the safe or known about the mustang. Once he had her lying on the backseat of the car, he went inside the house to join Gannon.

Gannon was currently searching through piles of paperwork that he had pulled out of a cabinet. "Any luck?" X asked.

Gannon looked up and pushed his glasses to the top of his head and nodded. He held out a piece of paper to X. He recognized the birth certificate when he looked down and noted that it was Lyric's but there was something off about it. X looked up at Gannon and frowned.

"What am I looking at, something isn't right," he said.

Gannon nodded his head, "yeah, it's a fake, a decent one, but there are just a few little things," he said pointing out the differences.

"Are there anymore in there?" X asked.

Gannon held out the three son's birth certificates, unlike Lyric's, the brothers, certificates were all real. When Gannon handed over Lyric's mothers certificate his mouth dropped open in surprise.

"What the fuck?" he said, his eyes widening in shock.

Gannon nodded and sighed, "she can't have known," he said.

X continued to look between Gannon and the certificates he held in his hand. Lyric's mother was one of Gable's sisters.

"But Gable would have known," X replied.

"Yeah, yeah he would have," Gannon said.

Steve came into the room and looked down at the certificates in Gannon's hand, his eyes widened as he read the name, "fuck," he spat, "this name, this woman, she ran, I thought she left town, do you remember Gannon?"

Gannon's eyes widened suddenly, and he nodded, "I do. The rumor was she fled in the middle of the night to get away from Gable's father, that's what spread the rumors about them inbreeding and fucking each other."

"Fuck," X said running his hands up over his face, "this is too much, how the fuck can this be even real life?"

"Lyric said that Gable took her because her father had something of Gable's, was it the drugs? The people in the trunk or the wife?" Gannon asked.

"I've got to assume it wasn't the wife, she said that there were bikers here getting their parts regularly, and you guys didn't use them, so it had to be Gable's crew. Which makes me wonder if Gable helped her mother escape, the rumors said that there was no way that she could have escaped without help, but no one could work out who," Steve explained.

"Then how the hell did she manage to stay hidden, what ten minutes away from her father, all this time?" X asked.

"Well that's the question isn't it? I've spoken to the chief, he is sending over a C.S.I unit to collect evidence, and the bodies. I won't know more until they have done their investigation, but once I do, I will let you guys know," Steve said.

"What about Lyric?" Gannon asked.

Steve nodded his head and sighed, "is she able to stay with you guys? She is over eighteen so C.P.S can't do anything to help, and this place will be a crime scene for the next little bit so she wouldn't be able to come back here, not that I think she would want to. She will have to give a statement as to what happened to her and where she has been, but I think she will be safer with you guys, than if we put her in police protection."

"She's staying with me," X said, leaving no room for argument. He wasn't going to allow her away from him. The minute that Gable realized that she was out there somewhere he would have been looking for her, once he realizes that she has spoken to the cops he is going to double his effort in finding her. Lyric's only chance at being safe was by X's side.

Nobody argued with X, they knew they weren't going to win. She was his, from that moment on, it didn't matter that he had only known her for three days, there was such a thing as love at first sight. Not that he was in love with Lyric, well not completely, she had managed to worm her way into his heart, but to say he was in love with her, that would take time. However, he cared enough about her that he wasn't going to let her go, that he wasn't going to leave her side and he wasn't going to leave her at the mercy of fucking Gable, and this fucked up family any longer.

The more that X thought about everything Gable had planned for her, his own damned biological niece, filled X with rage. He wanted to carve Gable to pieces. He shouldn't be surprised the rumor was that Gable's sons were as a result of incest, X didn't know if that was true, or whether people just said that because of Pitt. If Pitt hadn't been born with down syndrome, then the rumors might not be so rife. But surely Gable knew that Lyric was his sister's daughter, his niece. Then again, he never raped her, but why didn't he rape her? What was the point of waiting?

There were so many questions, so many loose ends. They needed to get hold of one of Gable's son's, someone in the inner circle, they needed information to find out exactly what the hell Lyric's father and brothers had going on and who the fuck Gable is in relation to her. X turned to Blaine and Gannon with a new sense of urgency.

"We need Pitt and Hawk; we need to talk to them. Pitt obviously cared for Lyric enough to bring her to us, maybe they can answer some of our questions," X said looking between Blaine, Gannon and Steve.

Steve frowned and shook his head, "do you think that Pitt would be able to answer the questions, I mean even despite his obvious disabilities, from all the rumors I've heard he was locked up tight there, he may know as little as Lyric does."

X hummed, Steve was right, Lyric told him that Pitt had been locked up in the room with her, and that was how she had got to know him, but unlike Lyric, Pitt still had some sense of freedom, he was allowed out on occasion under the care of Hawk. Lyric had mentioned that she had got the opportunity to get to know Hawk as well. And he would have had to be the one that was driving the car, so the two brothers were their best shot.

"Pitt might not know a lot, but Hawk will know more. And you know that wherever Pitt goes, Hawk goes. Hawk was the one that was driving that car, I would bet my left nut on it. If we can get both to open up to us, even for the sake of Lyric, then we will be able to find the answers, and maybe a kink in the chain that will help us to fix all of our problems."

"I hear what you're saying X and I like the idea of cutting the head off the snake, but I think there is another head just waiting to take over. Gable has been priming his sons since the day they were born. It won't matter if we take Gable out, we will have to take the entire family out, Pitt and Hawk included if we want to get rid of all of them," Blaine said with a sigh.

"Maybe, but what if Pitt and Hawk defected? What if we were able to offer them freedom, a place of safety where Pitt wouldn't be abused?" Gannon asked.

X's eyes widened; he loved the idea. If Pitt and Hawk were given a place where they were protected from their father's tyrannical rule, maybe then that would be enough to make the kink in the chain big enough for them to take Gable and the rest of them out. Not only for Bree's death, but for Lyric's abuse, for other countless girls like Lyric, for those people in the trunk, hell even for Pitt.

"We will talk about it when we get back, first let's get Lyric's stuff cleared out of here, and get her home," Blaine said as Arsen and Hale arrived in the truck ready to move Lyric's belongings out of the house.

X wandered over to the SUV with his mind running through scenarios and ideas in how to extract revenge and take the Iron Horsemen out for good. He looked in on Lyric who was still asleep. Her eyes closed and her blonde eye lashes sweeping her cheeks, her pink lips parted slightly as she inhaled and exhaled. He turned to look around at the property. From the outside no one would be able to tell what was going on here, no one would know that there were three people dead and rotting in the trunk of a mustang locked in a garage that could be seen from the road, or that in the basement of the auto shop, in a safe was the head of the owner's wife in a jar. X shuddered, evil seemed to pour from the very foundation of the buildings, even the land seeped with the blood and evil doings of those that lived here, and yet one blonde angel shed her light and somehow made this place a little better.

Chapter Fourteen

Lyric

When Lyric's eyes fluttered open, she realized she was back in the bed that she had first woken up in. The memory of sobbing, vomiting, falling asleep encased in X's arms filled her mind. Her mother's head in a jar, the rotting corpses in the trunk of her father's car. She wished for the numbness that came with sleep, she wished she could go back there, but now that she was awake, Lyric's mind was filled with questions, and memories. She analyzed everything, all the little parts of her life, every memory from her childhood, just to give her some indication that she subconsciously knew that her father and brothers were bad people, doing bad things.

Lyric wasn't sure how long she had laid awake in bed, when the door quietly opened, she looked over to see X coming into the room, when he realized that she was awake, his face broke out in a smile. One that lit up his whole face. He was beautiful.

"Good morning, did you sleep well?" he asked.

Lyric nodded her head and smiled, "I can't believe that I slept for as long as I did," she said quietly.

X chuckled, "you were out for the count, you didn't even stir when I carried you in here from the car. You have had a rough seven months and your body is still healing, so it's going to take some time. Take all the rest you need."

"Thank you, I would really like to have a shower if I could please?" she asked.

X's eyes widened and he nodded his head, "oh yeah, of course, I'll go and get Hadley or Angel to help you," he said turning for the door.

Lyric stopped X, "it's alright, if you can just help me to walk to the bathroom and stand by the door, I will be alright," she said.

Lyric couldn't explain it, but she trusted X implicitly. He had given her no reason to trust him and she knew that it was probably naive to put her trust in a man that she didn't know at all, but there was something about him, something that spoke to her. It was like they connected on an unseen level, deeper somehow. Lyric knew that X wouldn't purposely cause her harm, and although he had a tough exterior, and she didn't doubt that he had done bad things, she knew that those bad things were done for the right reason.

X seemed almost shy and coy as he helped Lyric to stand from the bed and guide her to the bathroom. He reached out and flipped the water of the shower on as the steam started to rise and dance throughout the room.

"Um, will you be okay now? I can go get Hadley or Angel if you need more help," he said, almost shy.

Lyric giggled, she didn't believe for a minute that he wasn't well experienced, and she knew that he wouldn't be unfamiliar with the sight of a female body. She shook her head, "I'm alright, if I need you, I will call out, I promise," she said with a smile.

X nodded again, before he turned and left the room, shutting the door behind him. Lyric giggled again, before she stripped off the clothes that she had worn the day before. She noticed the stain of vomit on her t-shirt and in her hair, crinkling her nose, she stepped in under the warm water, feeling it cascade down over her body. It was exactly what she needed. Her muscles that were sore still from seven months of inactivity started to ease with the hot water. Lyric closed her eyes and allowed the water to pour down over her face, soaking up the cleansing liquid. Once she washed her hair and body, she was exhausted, she couldn't believe how much just the act of showering took out of her.

By the time she got out of the shower and dried herself she was ready to fall back into bed and sleep for a week. Lyric wrapped the towel around her body and opened the bathroom door, she didn't want to put on the clothes that smelled like vomit and were dirty from the day before, but she didn't know if she had any other clothes to wear. At least if she hid under the blankets it wouldn't matter if she was naked. She snorted at herself at the thought of feeling shame about being naked, the whole time that Gable had her, she was forbidden to wear clothes.

As she came into the bedroom, X was sitting on a freshly made bed, he looked up and his eyes widened, "oh shit, I didn't think about clothes for you to wear. Um, Arsen and Hale, the prospects, brought your clothes back for you yesterday. They are just in boxes for now, I figured you could decide where you wanted to put them," he said waving his hands towards the boxes. "If you sit on the bed, and tell me what you want to wear, I can find it out for you."

Lyric nodded her head and sat on the bed, watching X as he opened the boxes that she hadn't noticed lined against one wall. "Can I just have a t-shirt and some yoga pants or something loose fitting, even pajamas would be good," she said grateful to Arsen and Hale for bringing her clothes back for her.

X nodded his head and found out a pair of pajamas that she loved to wear when she was at home. She smiled and took them from him, before he turned his back, giving her a chance to get dressed in the soft cotton, sleep shorts and t-shirt.

"You can turn around now, I'm dressed," she said, as she slid into the clean sheets.

X turned around and watched her, she looked up at him and gave him a smile. "Did the police find anything? Like who those people were?" she asked.

X came and sat on the edge of the bed. Lyric flipped the corner of the blanket back and tapped the bed, encouraging him to climb in. X seemed to ponder the decision for a moment, before he pulled his shoes off, dropping them to the floor and climbing in beside her. He pulled her into him, X's arms felt good around her and she lay her head on his chest, running her hands along the hard ridges of his abs. X inhaled a sharp breath, holding her wrist and stilling her movements. He leaned down and kissed the top of her head.

"It's too early to know who the people were, they have to do DNA tests or something to find them, but they won't know that for a while. Steve said that they found a lot of drugs and some other evidence of other things that were going on," he said.

Lyric felt that he was avoiding telling her what the other things were, she looked up at him with a frown, "what other things, Maverick?" she asked using his real name.

X met her eye and raised an eyebrow and gave her a small smirk, before shaking his head, "minx," he said with a chuckle.

Lyric giggled, using his real name had been an outright manipulation, one that he obviously picked up on immediately, "are you going to tell me?"

X sighed and ran his hand up through his hair, "it's bad sweetheart, are you sure that you want to know?"

Lyric nodded her head, it wasn't that she wanted to know, it's that she needed to know, she needed to know who the hell her father was, and why Gable felt it was alright to take her and torture her for seven months.

"We found yours and your families birth certificate, yours was a fake," he said gauging her reaction, she blinked at him and nodded her head. Lyric thought she should be more shocked, but after seeing three rotting bodies in her father's car the day before, nothing was shocking her anymore.

X cleared his throat before continuing, "we also found your mum's birth certificate, she was Gable's younger sister who went missing as a teenager. We aren't sure if Gable only just found out where she was and that is what he was looking for, or if he always knew where she was."

Lyric sucked in a breath; she was related to that piece of shit. Tears prickled at her eyes; she didn't want to be related to him. Life had dealt her a shit hand, a hand that it had hidden for at least seventeen years, because she never realized how shit she really had it.

There was a knock on the door, before it opened slightly. Arsen stuck his head around the corner and looked in at them, his face flushed, when he saw them in the bed together, causing Lyric to chuckle.

"We are dressed," she said.

Arsen chuckled and cleared his throat, "X, Blaine wanted me to let you know that the um," he said glancing quickly at Lyric, obviously not wanting to say anything in front of her, "the people that we were trying to get to come, are here."

"Thanks man. I'll be right out," X replied.

Arsen nodded before slipping back through the door and shutting it with a soft click behind him, "is that to do with my family?" she asked.

X looked pensive for a moment, like he didn't want to answer her, before finally he nodded his head and kissed her on the cheek, "yeah baby it is. I'll be able to tell you more later, but right now, I can't say much, understand?"

Lyric frowned, she didn't understand, if it had something to do with her family then she should know. X seemed to be able to read the look on her face, because he sighed and ran his hands up over his face before groaning.

"You are bad for my heart, baby, I swear," he groaned again. Lyric wasn't sure what he meant by that and shrugged her shoulder, "alright listen, if I tell you what is going on, I need you to promise me that you will stay in this room and not move from here until I say it's safe to do so, alright?"

Lyric frowned, "are you going to do something dangerous?" she asked.

X shook his head, "no, no, nothing like that, it's just that the people that are here, well we wanted to talk to them first, to ask them the questions we needed to find out before you saw them. If you were to see them or if they saw you, then they might not be as willing to speak with us," he explained.

Lyric didn't understand how it worked inside a bike club, but she nodded out her agreement to stay in the room regardless. She trusted X; she knew that he wouldn't do anything that would put her in danger. He leaned forward and kissed her on the forehead.

"Good girl, right, well Pitt and Hawk are here," he said.

Lyric sucked in a sharp breath and her eyes widened, "you're not going to hurt them, are you?" she asked concerned.

Pitt didn't do anything but save her, she didn't want him to be hurt, he was as much a victim of Gable as she had been. X shook his head and took her hand in his.

"No baby, we aren't going to hurt them, in fact they came here on their own when we asked. We just want to ask them questions. We figured that they would be the best bet we had to getting answers that we were stuck on, like why Gable never raped you, even though he kept threatening it and what he had planned with you and perhaps what it was that your dad and brothers were doing working for him," he explained.

Lyric relaxed glad that he wasn't going to hurt Pitt. She really had come to like him like a big brother while she had been in that concrete room, and Hawk had always made her laugh and she liked the way that he treated Pitt. She knew that he was protective of his brother and tried to prevent Gable from hurting him too badly. Sometimes though Gable was able to hurt Pitt when Hawk wasn't there to protect him.

"Once we have the information we need, and I know that Pitt and Hawk truly meant to keep you safe, then we will be able to bring them to you, so you can see them alright?" X said.

Lyric's eyes widened and her face broke out in a wide smile, "you promise?"

X chuckled and nodded his head, "yeah baby, I promise," he said slipping out of the bed and pulling his boots back onto his feet, before going to the door.

"I'll get Hadley to bring you in some food and maybe some of the girls can come keep you company if you like, or I'll get one of the prospects to set your television up for you," he said nodding his head at her television that was stacked in the corner.

Lyric smiled at him and nodded, "thank you Maverick," she said with a giggle.

X chuckled and shook his head, "minx."

Chapter Fifteen

X   When he left Lyric, it wasn't what he wanted to do. What he wanted to do was to curl up by her side and kiss her stupid. However, speaking with Pitt and Hawk was just as or if not more important than his sex drive. He went into the small room behind the bar that they used for meetings, and saw that Blaine and Gannon were already sitting on the couches, with Pitt curled into Hawks side on the other couch. When he opened the door and walked through Pitt looked up with wide eyes. The poor guy looked terrified. When he took note, X realized that Pitt was a lot younger than he first thought, he was only a kid himself, around the same age as Lyric.

Hawk wasn't a whole lot older, and looking at them, there was no question that they were brothers, with their stark light blonde hair and big blue eyes. X sat down on a chair beside Gannon and watched the boys. Pitt slipped his hand into Hawks and held onto him for dear life. X's heart seized at the movement. This was a kid, scattered with bruises, his eyes were blackened, and X could make out wounds dotting up his arms, he was a scared kid that had been born into a cruel world.

"Pitt?" X said quietly, the boy's head snapped up and he looked over at X with big eyes, his whole body was trembling with fear. "No one is going to hurt you here; we just want to talk to you. We won't touch you and won't let anyone touch you," X continued quietly.

Pitt continued to tremble, but he seemed to relax slightly as X's words sunk into him. Hawk watched X with narrowed eyes, this was a kid who had been taught not to trust and from the clutch that he had on Pitt, he would die protecting his brother.

"Why did you ask us to come here?" Hawk asked.

Blaine cleared his throat and sat forward slowly, so as not to alarm either boy, "first off, I want to thank you both for bringing Lyric here to us, we are keeping her safe and won't allow her to go back to your father."

Pitt's eyes widened and a goofy smile broke out across his face at the mention of Lyric, "she is my friend, I saved her," he said proudly, tapping on his chest.

Blaine chuckled and nodded his head, "you did, and you did the right thing."

"Is she still here?" Hawk asked.

"Yes, she is, she is healing, she was hurt and starved, and has a long road to recovery, but she is healing," Blaine answered as they watched Hawk take a sigh of what seemed like relief.

"What did you need from us?" Hawk asked.

"We want to find out why your dad took her? What he wanted with her. Lyric said that he planned to breed her, but he never raped her, and we don't understand why he waited," Blaine asked.

"Dad wanted to do bad things to her, but I wouldn't let him. He punched her when I wasn't allowed in the room, but I broke in the room and stopped him. I killed him," Pitt said from where he sat tucked into Hawks side

X's eyes widened; he had killed Gable. A sense of disappointment went through X, as much as he would be thrilled that Gable was dead, it hadn't been by his hand. Hawk gave Pitt's hand a squeeze and cleared his throat before sitting back in the chair and running his hands up through his hair.

"Our father," Hawk spat with what seemed like disgust, "took Lyric seven months ago with the intention of raping her to get her pregnant. The mistake he made was letting her befriend Pitt. She became his friend, and he as a result became protective of her."

Hawk looked over at Pitt who was staring off into the distance, before Hawk cleared his throat and turned to Pitt, "hey man, you want to put your music on for a little bit, while I talk to the guys?" he asked.

X frowned, Pitt nodded his head and gave Hawk a small smile. He seemed to know that Hawk wanted to talk to them without him hearing but was willing to do as his brother instructed without question. He slipped the headphones out of his pocket and put them in his ears, before Hawk handed Pitt his phone and he scrolled through what must have been a music app. Once Pitt was relaxed back into the couch, with his eyes closed and his head bopping to the tune, Hawk turned back to them.

"I don't like talking about our father in front of him, it upsets him. Ever since Pitt was about four years old, our dad used rape and torture to control Pitt. It was like he knew that Pitt one day was going to be bigger than him and he needed to make him afraid before that happened. So, Pitt received regular beatings and different men from the club would rape him, some so brutally that he couldn't sit for days at a time," Hawk said shaking his head with disgust.

"Once I got big enough, I started taking on more of the care of Pitt, keeping him away from my dad and the other men. Anyway, when dad brought Lyric back to the club house and locked her up, he locked her up in Pitt's room. He didn't consider that all that he had done to Pitt didn't turn him into a sexual deviant. Lyric and Pitt got to know one another, and Pitt became protective of her. I think dad was hoping that Pitt would rape her, and torture her to make her compliant, but that's not what happened. Instead anytime dad went into the room and made any attempt to either beat or even rape her, Pitt would protect her. He took a lot of the beatings at first.

Then dad started locking Pitt out of the room or sending him out with me in order to beat and torture her. I don't know why he didn't rape her during those times, but it seemed to have become some sort of game to him. To see how far he could push her before she became compliant to him. It never worked," Hawk said with a humorless chuckle and shake of his head.

"She is the strongest woman that I had ever met, stronger than any of the others that he took. Anyway, on that final day, Pitt overheard dad saying that he was going to just rape her, get it out of the way, that he had wasted enough time on her. Pitt flew into a rage and broke down the door to the room. A fucking huge steel fucking door, and Pitt was so angry he literally knocked the fucking thing off the frame. Dad had just knocked Lyric out and was about to take her, when Pitt got into the room and stabbed him in the neck. Pitt picked Lyric up and brought her to me, she was unconscious. It was his idea to bring her here. I don't even know how he knew about you guys, but he just kept telling me that we needed to bring her here, that you guys would protect her from dad. I don't think he realized that he killed him at first. Not until later that night when we got back, and Ace beat us so badly."

X sat with his mouth open and ran his hands up over his face. Fucking hell. What a fucking nightmare. But he couldn't express how grateful he was for Pitt and Hawk, for protecting his girl.

"Has Ace taken over?" Gannon asked.

Hawk looked over at him and nodded his head before sighing, "he is worse than what dad ever was, he is eviler," he said with a shake of his head.

"What did Lyric's father have of Gable's that caused him to take her in the first place?" X asked, drawing Hawk's attention to him.

"Macca was married to my aunty. It was a secret, she ran away after she got pregnant with Clint, Lyric's older brother. I heard my dad say once that my grandfather had beaten her badly when he found out she was pregnant and was demanding that she get rid of the baby, so she took off to live with Macca. Dad was the one that helped her to escape and he was the only one that knew where she was. He made sure that Macca never let her off the property, so that our grandfather didn't see her. Dad and Macca had been childhood friends, they grew up together, so it was natural that Macca started working with dad when he took over the club," Hawk explained.

"What kind of work were they doing?" Blaine asked.

"Mostly drugs, but when dad took over the club, he wanted to get into sex trafficking. He would take women, so that he could grow the club, but he would sell some of them, to other guys out of town," Hawk answered.

X frowned and chewed on his lip, "so the stories about inbreeding? All of it wasn't true?" he asked.

Hawk chuckled and shook his head, "no, that was a rumor that dad spread. He didn't want the community looking too closely at us, so he figured if the town believed that all the babies that were being born, were conceived by incest then people would look the other way. It helped when Pitt was born with down syndrome, people saw him and just assumed it was true. Once the women raised the children and were no good to them anymore, dad would kill them and get new ones. Macca and his sons oversaw kidnapping the girls and bringing them back."

"So, was it drugs or girls that Macca had that Gable was looking for?" Blaine asked.

"Girls, Brenton had been on a trip to pick up their latest load of girls, but when he got back Macca told dad that he wasn't handing them over, that they had decided to keep them because Lyric wasn't going to be any good to them," Hawk answered.

"What does that mean?" Gannon asked.

"Lyric was stolen as a baby," Hawk said looking at the shocked looks on all three men's faces. "I didn't know that either until after dad took her. I heard him telling Ace one night. Apparently, the plan had been that once Lyric was fifteen, Macca was supposed to give her to Clint to start breeding with, but when Lyric's mum found out what was going to happen, she threatened to go to the police. When she made the threat, Macca lost his mind and killed her, beating her to death."

X frowned, Lyric believed that her mum died of cancer, and yet the whole time her mum, who wasn't even her biological mum, had been killed at the hands of the man that she believed to be her father.

"So why didn't Clint fuck Lyric after her mum's death?" Blaine asked.

Hawk winced at the crass term that Blaine used before he shrugged his shoulders, "I don't know, dad was under the impression that he had, but when she didn't get pregnant, he assumed that she was broken."

X shook his head, "she is still a virgin," he stated.

Hawks eyes widened, "oh, wow," he said.

"So, Lyric's dad and brothers took these girls and weren't going to hand them over to Gable?" Gannon asked, bringing them back on track.

Hawk sighed and nodded his head, "yeah, he wanted more girls to start producing children, for Ace and Axe. I didn't want anything to do with it. I hated everything my father did. I hated my father. I'm glad the cunt is dead. Anyway, Macca refused to hand over the girls, or the money that he got for them, so dad went to get them back. When he saw Lyric, he decided at the last minute instead that he would take her, however, when Macca and the boys came in from work, dad said they didn't give a shit that he had taken Lyric. Apparently, Macca just shrugged his shoulders and said easy come, easy go."

"Fuck," X spat, if that fucker wasn't already dead, he would go there and kill him immediately, "where did Lyric come from?"

"I asked dad that, he said that Macca bought her off some junkies that he used to deal to," he said with a humorless chuckle, "fucking sold their kid for a gram of fucking coke."

"Well, what do you want to do now? I'm willing to have you and Pitt here with us and give you safety. You can defect from the Iron Horsemen and join here," Blaine said.

"We aren't members of the Iron Horsemen anyway, we were never allowed to join, because Pitt's disabilities and because I'm defective, according to my father."

X didn't know what that meant, that he was defective and figured that was a question for another time.

"Do you want to stay here?" Blaine asked.

Hawk nodded his head, "we aren't safe over there, the beatings are getting worse, life will only be worse under Ace. Pitt and I won't live for long there. So, if you at the very least promise to keep Pitt safe then I am happy to stay here."

"That's easy. I can promise that. You nor Pitt will be beat living here. We are a family, not a fucking dictatorship, evil cult," Blaine said.

Hawk nodded his head and tapped Pitt on the shoulder, when Pitt took his earphones out, he looked at Hawk with a huge smile on his face.

"Blaine, Gannon and X asked if we wanted to stay with them now, instead of with Ace. I said I wanted to stay; do you want to?" Hawk asked.

Pitt's eyes widened and his face broke out in the most startling smile, that lit up his entire face, before nodding his head emphatically. He turned to look between Blaine, Gannon and X and smiled broadly.

"Yes, I want to stay here. Can Lyric stay here too?" he asked.

X chuckled, it seemed that his girl had that effect on everyone, "yeah Lyric is staying here too. Do you want to see her?"

Pitt's eyes widened even more. X didn't think the boy could smile anymore widely than he already was, but he proved him wrong. His head bobbed up and down excitedly. "Yes please. She's my friend."

"Well come on then, let me take you to where she is resting, and you can see her," X said standing from his chair, and encouraging Pitt and Hawk to follow him.

Pitt followed without question, but Hawk was a little more dubious, obviously not trusting X completely. He understood Hawk's fear. As they walked down the hallway towards the bedroom that Lyric was in, Pitt talked wildly about Lyric and how much he liked her and how they would play cards or that she would sing to him when he was sad. X reached out and knocked on the door to the bedroom and listened for Lyric to call out.

He opened the door and walked into the room, with Pitt and Hawk close on his heels, "hey sweetheart, I brought some friends of yours that wanted to see you," he said with a chuckle.

"Lyric," Pitt cried, before running past X and leaping onto the bed beside her, gently pulling her into a hug and holding her tight.

X's mind wanted to seize with jealousy, but he stamped it out quickly. Pitt was like an excited, oversized toddler. He had nothing to be jealous of. Lyric was still his girl. Lyric chuckled as she hugged Pitt close to her. Her eyes were filled with tears as she looked over his body, noticing all the bruises on his skin.

"Oh Pitt, what did they do to you?" she said sadly.

Chapter Sixteen

Lyric

What had they done to Pitt? He was covered in bruises and old wounds. That poor sweet boy, he didn't have an evil bone in his body, and yet he had been so mistreated all his life. It made Lyric sick when she thought about what he had been through.

"I'm alright Lyric. Dad is dead now. And X, he said me, and Hawk can stay here with you," Pitt said excitedly.

Lyric's eyes widened and she looked up over Pitt's shoulder to X, who confirmed what Pitt was saying with a nod of his head.

"That's wonderful, I'm so glad that you are staying here, I've missed seeing your face," she said, "thank you for saving me Pitt."

She leaned forward and kissed him on the forehead. He smiled and puffed out his chest. He was proud and that's exactly how she wanted him to feel. Lyric looked over at Hawk who was standing off towards the door looking uncomfortable.

"Hey Hawk," she said with a warm smile.

"Hey Lyric, I'm glad that you are okay," he said.

She giggled and nodded her head, "I'm okay, because of you and Pitt. Thank you."

Hawk waved his hand, "you don't have to thank us Lyric; we did what was right," he said.

Lyric shook her head, "you did what was right, sure, but you went against your family to do it. That is a brave act, not something too many other people would do," she replied.

Hawk gave her a smile, while Pitt continued to hold her close to his chest and stroke her hair, as if he was too afraid to let her go, in case she disappeared on him. She let out a big yawn that clicked her jaw and felt the exhaustion that seemed to be ever present lately start to take over. Hawk noticed how tired she was and tapped Pitt on the shoulder.

"Come on buddy, let's go and let Lyric get some sleep, her body is still getting better, we can come see her when she wakes up later, alright?" Hawk said.

Pitt looked down at Lyric and back over at Hawk, "promise?" he asked.

"I promise," Hawk said with a smile.

Pitt nodded and gave her a big wet kiss on the forehead before he stood up and followed Hawk out the door, letting it shut behind them. Lyric couldn't wipe the smile off her face, to know that Blaine, Gannon and X said that they could stay there, that they would be away from their family's rules, meant the world to her. They were safe now. And knowing that Gable was dead, made her feel weirdly satisfied, like she had already got revenge, without even realizing it.

X kicked his boots off and reached for his belt. Lyric's eyes widened as she watched him undo the button of his jeans and shuck them off, so that he stood in just a t-shirt and boxers. He wordlessly slipped into the bed beside her and pulled her into his chest. Lyric reached up and ran her fingers up through his beard, feeling her eyes drift shut.

"Did you get the answers you were looking for?" she asked.

"Yes, baby, it's not good," he said.

Lyric nodded her head, "I didn't think it would be," she sighed, "but will you tell me?"

X looked down at her with a frown on his face before nodding and delving into everything that Hawk had told them. X hadn't lied, it wasn't good, it was horrible, and Lyric's heart was breaking. Her mother had died at the hand of her father. And to make matters worse they weren't even her biological parents. Instead her biological parents had sold her for drugs as a baby. She couldn't believe the fucked-up world that she had unknowingly been born into and wondered what she had done to deserve such a life.

Lyric lay there silently running her fingers casually through X's beard, as sleep took over her. It didn't matter now where her life had been, or who she came from All that mattered now was where it was headed. Her life could only get better.

She didn't know how long she had been asleep for, but when she flicked her eyes open, it was to see Pitt watching her, like he had when she was locked in the room with him. Hawk was sitting in the chair beside the bed, while Pitt sat on the floor watching her sleep. To some it might have creeped them out, and at first it had Lyric. But she soon took comfort in Pitt's nuances. This wasn't Pitt being creepy, this was Pitt protecting her, keeping her safe.

"Hey there," she whispered.

"Good morning Lyric," he said with a smile.

"It's morning?" she asked.

Pitt beamed a grin at her and nodded his head, "you slept all day and night, you must have been super tired. Hawk said it was because your body is still getting better."

"Yeah, it is, but soon I will be well again and then I can spend more time awake and we can watch some movies or something together and play cards," she said with a smile.

Pitt bobbed his head with excitement causing her to giggle, she looked up at Hawk who was watching them fondly.

"What did you two get up to yesterday?" she asked.

"We helped Blaine, Gannon, X, Arsen and Hale take over the Iron Horsemen. And guess what? The police came, they arrested Ace and Axe and some of the others, and l the girls that dad took they went back to their homes, we saved them Lyric," Pitt said with a huge grin.

Lyric's eyes widened. Did that mean that the Iron Horsemen were no longer in existence? She looked up at Hawk, and he nodded in confirmation.

"I would have liked to blow the entire building up, but it wasn't fair to the kids or the women. But there have been police, not just local police either, combing all over the town and uncovering everything. X said they even arrested some of the cops who were on dad's payroll," Hawk told her with excitement in his voice.

This was the best news that she could ever hear. The door opened and X came in wearing a big smile, "hey baby, I take it Pitt and Hawk just told you the good news?" he said with a chuckle.

"Yeah, they did, that is fantastic news, I'm thrilled. What does it mean for all of us though?" she asked.

"Well Blaine, Gannon and I have been talking, and we all decided that if you want to stay here with us, we would love to have you here. There is a lawyer coming to see you in the next few days. Once the police have released the property from their investigation, it will be transferred to your name, to do whatever you want with it," X said.

Lyric frowned, she didn't want the property, "just pull the building down and build a park or something on it, sell it, hell I don't care, I want nothing to do with it," she said firmly.

X smiled and nodded, "I thought you might say something like that," he chuckled, "so would you like to stay here with me, sweetheart?"

Lyric smiled, "yeah I would," she said.

She wanted to explore what there was between her and X, she felt so safe with him and with Pitt and Hawk staying, she knew there was nowhere else she would be willing to be. Even if nothing came from her and X, she looked at Pitt and Hawk like they were brothers, they had been through so much together, which brought them intrinsically closer than just friends and there was nothing that would keep her from staying by their side.

X leaned over Pitt's shoulder, pressing a kiss to her forehead, "I'm glad because I would have hated to have to beg," he grinned.

Lyric laughed. It felt good, it felt freeing. Their life was on the precipice of change. It was a change for the better. She looked between the three guys in the room with her, they had been brought together by tragedy, but it was only going to be a blip in their life. Their future from here on out was all that mattered. And Lyric could feel it in her soul, their future owed them some good times.

X turned to Hawk with a small frown on his brow, "Hawk you said something yesterday, and I wanted to ask what you meant by it. You said that your dad thought you were defective? Why?" he asked.

Hawk chuckled and shook his head, "I'm transgendered," he said. Both Lyric's and X's eyes widened as they watched Hawk laugh, "I've been on testosterone therapy for the past two years, since I turned eighteen, to transition from a female to a male," he explained.

"Holy shit," X said, his eyes still wide, "I would never have fucking guessed that, well shit man, there is nothing fucking defective about that. You are you, I don't give a shit whether you have a cock and balls or a pussy, if you tell me you are a man, then that is what you are. Your genitalia aren't my business," he said.

Lyric was thrilled to see X be so accepting, she could only imagine how hard it was to transition as it was, but to do it under the rule of someone like Gable, it must have been hell.

"Thank you for telling us, not that you had to. But you are still as much my brother as Pitt is," she said.

Tears welled in Hawk's eyes and he nodded his thanks.

"You said that your dad wanted you to breed, I just assumed that you meant, that he was expecting you to breed with the women he stole, but that wasn't the case was it?" X asked.

Hawk quickly looked between Lyric and X before shaking his head, "no, I was supposed to be sold to Lachie."

"Fuck," Lyric spat with a shake of her head, "I'm glad all those pieces of shit are dead."

"Me too," Hawk whispered.

"You are safe now," X said giving Hawk's shoulder a small squeeze, "you don't have to tell a single soul as to what genitalia you were born with, you never have to speak about it again if you don't want to. But I will have your back if you do choose to tell anyone. You are safe here now. No one can touch you, that you don't give permission to."

Hawk shook his head, "man you guys run this club fucking different to the Iron Horsemen," he said with a bitter laugh.

"That's why we will be forever operational, and the Iron Horsemen are now nothing," X replied with a wry grin.

It was true. The Kingsmen, were different, admittedly, Lyric didn't know a lot about bike clubs or bikers in general, which was slightly laughable considering everything that had come to light in the last few days. However, what she did know was that they weren't as mean as they looked. She wasn't naïve enough to believe that they didn't do bad things, but when you were accepted, then you truly became family. And it's true what they say, sometimes you get the opportunity to pick your family.

Lyric couldn't have thought of a better family that she would be given the opportunity to pick.

The end.

Don't miss out!

Visit the website below and you can sign up to receive emails whenever S L Davies publishes a new book. There's no charge and no obligation.

https://books2read.com/r/B-A-NZRR-UFIDC

BOOKS 2 READ

Connecting independent readers to independent writers.

Did you love *Executioner*? Then you should read *Lynx*[1] by S L Davies!

[2]

Lynx is determined to bring down the seven Morpheus leaders. He has his in. Set to take over his father Louis Santos's position, Lynx knows it's time to act. Despite the AJE Authority demanding he wait. Lynx doesn't want to wait. How many more kids are going to die, be sold or abducted in the meantime. He is surrounded in the training facility by the Devil's Advocates. He knows he can beat them. Now is the time to act.Colt didn't want to work for Morpheus. He definitely didn't want to work at the training facility. But it was the best that he could hope for. Being born an omega in a breeding facility, it was either be bred by any countless number of alphas or hope that you got chosen to work for Morpheus. Colt knew he should feel lucky that he was chosen. But he hated it.

---

1. https://books2read.com/u/4Av7Kk

2. https://books2read.com/u/4Av7Kk

Also by S L Davies

Breeding Facility
Memphis
Bacchus
Coltrane
Pax
Raiden
Nash
Breeding Facility

Devil's Advocates
Lynx
Israel
Jai
Jasper
Arley
Zion
Oakland

KINK
Gunner

Newlyn

Aina

Freya

Tanquil

Obsidian Mechanics

Donte

Atticus

Boden

Onyx Rebels

Onyx Rebels Prologue

Hawke

Rison

Bandit

Butler

Nova

Rigby Brothers

Asher

Burgess

Macklin

Drake

Jericho

Obsidian

Schiavu
Schiavu

Shifter Ink
Brenton
Chase
Orion
Sloane

Stolen
Stolen
The Murphy Princess
Little Warrior

Wild Claw Pack
Connell

Standalone
Sisters Revenge
Killer Love
Soldiers At War
Second Chances
Bunny
Caged

By The Sword
The Cult
Rising Sun
Forbidden Bound
Christmas Escape
Executioner

Watch for more at https://www.amazon.com/~/e/B0832T8F7Z.

About the Author

S L Davies is an Australian Author living in Country, Victoria. She is inspired by the world around her.

Read more at https://www.amazon.com/~/e/B0832T8F7Z.

www.ingramcontent.com/pod-product-compliance
Lightning Source LLC
Chambersburg PA
CBHW031349160726
47993CB00002B/888